HORUS
AND THE CURSE OF
EVERLASTING REGRET

HORUS

AND THE CURSE OF

EVERLASTING REGRET

HANNAH VOSKUIL

Alfred A. Knopf
New York

THIS IS A BORZOI BOOK PUBLISHED BY ALFRED A. KNOPF

Visit us on the Web! randomhousekids.com

Educators and librarians, for a variety of teaching tools, visit us at RHTeachersLibrarians.com

Library of Congress Cataloging-in-Publication Data
Names: Voskuil, Hannah.
Title: Horus and the curse of everlasting regret / Hannah Voskuil.
Description: First edition. | New York : Alfred A. Knopf, [2016] | Summary: In 1934, hoping to earn the $1,000 reward they both need, young Peter and Tunie team up with Tunie's bat, Perch, and an Egyptian boy, Horus, cursed and mummified at age ten, to find a ten-year-old missing girl, Dorothy James.
Identifiers: LCCN 2015018121 | ISBN 978-1-101-93333-6 (trade) |
ISBN 978-1-101-93334-3 (lib. bdg.) | ISBN 978-1-101-93335-0 (ebook)
Subjects: | CYAC: Mystery and detective stories. | Missing children—Fiction. |
Mummies—Fiction. | Bats—Fiction. | Blessing and cursing—Fiction.
Classification: LCC PZ7.1.V68 Hor 2016 | DDC [Fic]—dc23
LC record available at http://lccn.loc.gov/2015018121?

Printed in the United States of America
August 2016
10 9 8 7 6 5 4 3 2 1

First Edition

For Karl, my beloved husband and tireless champion—
you deserve a medal. You get this dedication.

HORUS
AND THE CURSE OF
EVERLASTING
REGRET

CHAPTER 1

Harbortown, 1934

Peter balanced on the tilting fire escape behind the schoolhouse. The rusting iron platform overlooked the alley, and if he leaned out far enough, Peter could see the intersection of the alley and the busy street. His twin stepbrothers, Larry and Randall, still loitered there. Larry leaned against a streetlamp, tossing something up and down. He squinted upward from beneath his flat cap, caught sight of Peter, and waved.

Rats, thought Peter. A tin bucket sat at Larry's feet. There couldn't be anything good in it. The hulking Randall was hunched over beside his twin brother and poking a stick at something on the brick sidewalk.

Peter's gangly teacher, Miss Baker, banged open the classroom door. Peter began clapping together the forgotten erasers vigorously. The air filled with floury chalk dust.

"Thank you for volunteering to clean up, Peter," Miss Baker said, smiling. "Everyone else seemed in a hurry to begin summer recess."

"I don't mind, ma'am," said Peter honestly, though he could feel the prickling crawl of sweat gathering at his temples. Lately, he'd been experiencing a kind of creeping expectancy, an uneasy apprehension that had him flinching at shadows. He supposed it was the cumulative effect of his stepbrothers' pranks, or dread of the summer to come.

"Well, I appreciate it." Miss Baker's head bobbed on her long neck in a nod of approval. She ducked back into the classroom. Some of the other kids in his class made fun of Miss Baker—they called her the Ostrich—but Peter liked her. Earlier in the year, she'd seen Peter sharing his noon dinner with Tommy Barclay, whose family could not afford even the penny lunch. The next day, she'd asked Tommy to help her with classroom setup every afternoon in exchange for school luncheon. Peter was pretty sure she didn't really need Tommy's help. Best of all, Miss Baker had never given Peter that phony speech like every other grown-up, about how nice it must be to have a stepmother and siblings now, a real family. Miss Baker seemed to know it was about as nice as being tied in a sack with a couple of feral weasels.

Peter loosened his school tie and cast one final glance over the iron railing. He'd hoped if he took long enough to leave, Larry and Randall would tire of waiting for him and go find someone else to torment. No such luck.

"Is there anything else I can do?" Peter asked Miss Baker hopefully, back in the classroom.

"We've finished. I'm just going to take a last look around and lock up."

Peter went downstairs to the lobby and dawdled inside the windowed schoolhouse door. He gazed out past his pale reflection at the motorcars and trolleys and occasional horse passing on the street. He couldn't see his stepbrothers from here, but he knew they were around the corner. Just once, he'd like to walk past the twins with a friend at his side. No one was brave enough.

Since baseball season ended, his stepbrothers had had nothing better to do after school than lie in wait for Peter. Randall was built like a buffalo. Larry, the cleverer of the two, was bony and hard-hearted. They both had the manners of animals.

Miss Baker descended the steps, carrying a milk crate full of students' misplaced items. She peered down at them.

"What a shame. Ginger left her beautiful new coat and hat." Miss Baker held up a yellow flowered raincoat. Peter quickly saw an opportunity.

"I'll take them to her," he said.

"That's very kind, thank you." Miss Baker handed him the coat and wide-brimmed matching hat, and Peter made a show of neatly folding the coat and placing it carefully in his knapsack.

They parted ways at the bottom of the steps. Peter pretended to tie his shoe until Miss Baker melded into the busy throng on the sidewalk. Then he unbuckled his bag and withdrew the coat.

He wished it were less girlish. The bright daffodil pattern was discouragingly eye-catching, and the coat was inappropriate for this cloudless day. Still, as a disguise it might work. His stepbrothers would be scanning for Peter's familiar school clothes. All Peter needed was to get by them; he was faster than the twins, and with a head start he'd beat them over the bridge and back to the brownstone.

Peter pulled on Ginger's raincoat. The sleeves were too short and the armpit seams snug. He tugged the hat down as low as possible and joined the crowd waiting to cross at the traffic light. He felt as silly as a walking banana and prayed he wouldn't run into anyone he knew. Once on the far side of the street, he hurried up the block in the twins' direction. At the very least, they'd have to cross traffic to reach him. In recent months, that had helped, sometimes.

Peter didn't dare look over to where Larry and Randall were lurking. Instead, he turned toward the notices posted in the shop windows, walking at a clip past advertisements for Croft Ale and the new 1934 Ford Deluxe. Then one poster in particular caught his eye. Across the top it said MISSING: DOROTHY JAMES. Beneath it was a description: "Ten years old, curly dark hair, brown eyes, heart-shaped birthmark on left forearm. Last seen May 14, at the Harbortown Fairgrounds' *Mummies of Ancient Egypt* exhibit, wearing a light blue dress and matching ribbon headband."

Peter had overheard some of his classmates who'd gone to the fair. Everyone agreed that exhibit was eerie. One boy said even though he was alone in the mummy tent, he'd felt like someone was waiting in the shadows. Peter was thinking about this when he spied what was written across the bottom of the notice: $1,000 REWARD OFFERED FOR INFORMATION LEADING TO DOROTHY'S SAFE RETURN.

"A thousand dollars!" Peter said aloud. Whoops. No need to draw attention; he pulled the rain hat lower and resumed his march. *I would do almost anything for that money!* His father was leaving soon to conduct studies on alkaline batteries with some other engineering professors in New York City, and his stepmother mostly ignored him. With school out and only the short-tempered housekeeper, Miss Cook, to look out for him, he'd be at the twins' mercy all summer. He'd have only his robot, WindUp, for company.

For the hundredth time, Peter wished he were leaving for Camp Contraption, a residential summer camp in the far-off Blue Ridge Mountains. When he'd discovered it, he'd pleaded with his father to send him. Two and a half months of nature hikes and engineering—the campers even built their own automatons!—sounded like a dream come true. But a dream it was—a $200 dream his family couldn't afford.

It was settled. Peter would stay home with the twins for what he had begun to think of as the Summer of Doom.

"Hey!" A sharp, high voice interrupted Peter's thoughts. With dismay, Peter looked up into the wide green eyes of none other than the redheaded Ginger Hall, whose yellow flowered coat and hat Peter was currently modeling. "That's my coat!" She looked Peter over, aghast. "It looks terrible on you!"

Peter's face grew hot. Ginger was causing a small stir on the sidewalk. A barber and his client watched them through a window. A tall man in a porkpie hat who'd been walking his dog regarded Peter and frowned. Ginger's mother opened her mouth but seemed unable to think of anything to say.

"Shh! Here! Sorry!" Blushing, Peter awkwardly tore off the coat and hat, thrusting them into Ginger's hands. "I was bringing them to you, I just . . ."

Both Ginger and her mother looked appalled, but Peter had no time to explain. There was a squeal of tires, and Peter saw his stepbrother Randall vaulting over the hood of an automobile toward them, his broad face the very picture of wicked glee.

Peter took flight. His stepbrothers dashed after him.

"Excuse me! Pardon! Coming through!" Peter shouted. He dodged pedestrians on the fenced sidewalk portion of the bridge, and squeezed past a large man in a bowler who'd paused to observe the boats on the river. Peter didn't dare look back. His knapsack thumped against his spine as he pelted down the last stretch of the bridge and onto the street.

Whizz! A stinky projectile flew past Peter's peripheral vision. Peter turned the corner at full speed, nearly knocking over a postman. Something smashed into the tree branches near his head, and Peter ducked.

"Dog bombs away!" Randall shouted with unrestrained joy as what appeared to be a brown snowball exploded near Peter's feet. Dog bombs were Larry's invention, a mixture of mud and dog droppings, rolled into apple-sized balls. Their odor was atrocious.

Peter was only one block from their brownstone, but an Oshkosh truck with a bed full of fruit crates blocked the intersection. He had no choice—he would have to use his emergency plan.

He veered left down the block and into a semi-vacant lot where the charred remains of a burned-out bakery stood. Behind him, Randall tripped on the nearly invisible fishing line Peter had stretched between a fallen beam and a metal pole. Randall sprawled, dirt billowing up into the air around him. Larry stepped over the line, picked up a rolling dog bomb, and continued the chase.

Peter sprinted away and back across the now-empty

street. Their brownstone was in sight. He leaped up the stairs. The front door swung open just as he reached the top step. A dog bomb splattered on the sidewalk in front of the stoop. Larry had an impressive throwing arm. Peter's father frowned and peered up at the sky absentmindedly.

"Forgot to get the morning paper," he said, leaning down to pick up the newspaper from the step. "There's a letter on the hall table for you. Make sure you stop in and say hello to your stepmother."

Peter wiped the sweat from his forehead and dutifully went to the parlor. He greeted his stepmother in a rush.

"Hi, Stepma," he said, using their agreed-upon name. She was rocking baby Lucy, whose eyes were pinched with wailing. Peter spied Lucy's favorite stuffed bunny under the tea table. Still trying to catch his breath, Peter threw off his knapsack, dropped to his knees, and grabbed the bunny. He held the ratty toy up to Lucy's soft arms.

"Here you go, Luce," he said. She grasped the bunny and stuffed it into her mouth, blinking at him. Peter ran out the door and was halfway up the stairs when he realized he'd left his knapsack in the parlor.

Peter hurried to retrieve the pack, bolted back up the stairway, and was outside the door to his room when Larry emerged from across the hall. *Rats!* Larry's thin face was coated with a fine layer of dirt. He narrowed his pink-rimmed eyes and lunged for Peter.

"Gotcha!" Larry said with an evil sneer.

CHAPTER 2

Tunie stopped at the back door of Eleanor's Elegant Sweet Shoppe and tugged up each drooping kneesock. The socks had once been white but now were tinged gray from wear. She lifted her pet bat, Perch, from her shoulder and set him gently on a dripping pipe that stuck out from the building. Perch spun until he was hanging upside down, his black wings closing around him. He did not look pleased to be left behind in the dank alley, which smelled like ripe old garbage and mop water.

"Sorry, Perch, but you know how it is. Not everyone loves a bat."

He closed his eyes, indignant. Perch was unusual to a spooky degree. Most people wouldn't believe Tunie if she told them what he could do, or that she had a sort of sense for such unusual things.

She sighed and smoothed back the hair that had slipped from her brown braid, tucking it under the light blue ribbon headband Perch had found. There was no time to plait her hair again; she was late already. She opened the back door to the kitchen.

"What are you doin' here?" A round-cheeked new baker looked Tunie over, taking in the sagging socks, the broken shoelace, the frayed hem of the skirt. The baker lifted a wooden spoon. "Out! Shoo!" she said, for all the world, as if Tunie were a pigeon.

Tunie took a step back, and as she tried to explain, Miss Eleanor strode into the kitchen. She shut the door to the shop behind her, keeping the fancy customers out of view.

"It's all right, Marge. This is Petunia. She is our calligraphist." Miss Eleanor turned and climbed the flight of stairs to the business office, expecting Tunie to follow, which she did. Marge's sour expression said what she thought of Eleanor's taste in calligraphists. Tunie resisted the urge to stick out her tongue and scrambled to keep up with Miss Eleanor's fine silk skirt.

"You're late," Miss Eleanor said sternly over her shoulder.

"I'm sorry, ma'am, there was—"

"Never mind," Miss Eleanor interrupted. "I'm in a rush. Clean your hands and I'll show you today's work."

"Yes, ma'am."

Miss Eleanor stacked ivory cards on the glossy wooden desk that nearly filled the closet-sized office. She hunted around in a stack of papers while Tunie washed her hands at the small sink. It was one of Tunie's favorite parts of the job—washing with the sweet, rose-scented soap. Tunie carefully dried her hands and rolled up her sleeves.

Miss Eleanor impatiently waved Tunie to the padded leather desk chair. "I've left the cards and the list here. I'll be back in half an hour to check on your progress."

Miss Eleanor departed in a swirl of skirts. Tunie took a moment to breathe in the delicious smell of blueberry scones baking below and to appreciate the vine-patterned wallpaper. Then she bent over the thick rectangular cards and began carefully copying the names of next week's specials: *Strawberry Torte, Powdered Lemon Drops, Chocolate Hazelnut Wafers.*

Before she died of cholera, Tunie's mother had been an artist. She'd taught Tunie how to sketch, how to paint, and—most valuably—how to write in beautiful, elegant script. This last skill was what Miss Eleanor paid Tunie to do. She'd spied a HELP WANTED sign in Miss Eleanor's shop window a few months earlier. For writing out the names of the bakery specials for the store display, Miss Eleanor gave Tunie a few coins and a bag of day-old baked goods. It wasn't much, but there were times when the stale biscuits and hard scones were all Tunie and her father had to eat.

Tunie had just finished the last mouthwatering

flourish on *Bacon Cheddar Scones* when she heard a screech at the window. Tunie glanced up in time to see Perch, his black wings flapping frantically against the pane. He dove away just as a large striped tomcat on the rooftop pounced, hitting the window with a thud.

"Perch!" Tunie cried. She leaped to her feet. The stack of cards scattered and the Moore fountain pen dropped to the floor. Tunie hurried to the window, stepping on the pen, which broke with a crack. She yanked on the sash. It was stuck. Tunie pulled with all her might until it opened a mere three inches. Perch flew in with a shriek. The tomcat yowled on the windowsill and stretched a paw into the room as far as it could.

"What is the meaning of this?!" Miss Eleanor hissed in the doorway. Her pointy, powdered features were pinched with displeasure. "All the customers downstairs can hear you screeching and thumping!"

"There's . . . ," Tunie improvised hurriedly, "a bat! In here!"

"What?" Miss Eleanor's eyes widened as she turned around. Tunie motioned for Perch to come out and show himself.

Miss Eleanor put her hands on her hips. "I don't see any— *Eeeeek!*"

Perch flew down and flapped around Miss Eleanor's head a few times before disappearing behind a bookcase. She ducked and flailed her arms in an unladylike fashion.

Tunie said, "I can get him out, ma'am."

"Well, be quick about it!" Miss Eleanor swiftly made her way to the door. "And for goodness' sake, don't tell the customers!"

She fled down the stairs.

Tunie tidied up her work space. At least she hadn't stepped on the cards, though the broken pen would surely leak now.

She opened the small drawstring bag she carried.

"Hop in, Perch," she said. Perch landed on the desk but made no move to get in the pouch.

"I know you don't like it, but Miss Eleanor's upset! I need to tell her you're gone, or we won't get a plugged nickel for this work. I'll open the bag the moment we're outside, honest."

Perch took a few mincing steps toward Tunie and then reluctantly stepped into the bag. He peered grumpily up at Tunie from inside.

"You are the very finest bat," Tunie whispered to him warmly. She glanced around, went to the window, and shut it. Then she opened the door and called quietly to Miss Eleanor.

Miss Eleanor appeared at the foot of the stairs. "Well?"

"It's . . . gone. I got it with a book and dropped it out the window."

A look of distaste crossed Miss Eleanor's face, and she ascended the stairs and pushed past Tunie back into the room. She peered at the cards.

"Good enough, I suppose," she said of the elegant flourishes, the gorgeous lettering. Then she spied the pen and lifted it up to inspect it. A large crack ran down the side. "How on earth did you do that?"

"I stepped on it when the bat startled me," Tunie replied. Bat, cat. It didn't matter, really.

"Well, that will come out of your pay." Miss Eleanor pulled out her change purse and counted out two fewer coins than usual into Tunie's hand. "I left your bag of day-olds on the counter by the door. You may pick it up on your way out."

Tunie hid her dismay at the reduced pay and thanked Miss Eleanor. She hurried down the stairs, snatching her bag of day-olds as she left.

Perch began squeaking the moment Tunie stepped outside, and continued even after Tunie released him from her bag.

"I know, I know," Tunie said. "The pen wasn't my fault. I can't argue with her, though, Perch. You can't eat arguments, even winning ones. Come on—the apothecary closes in ten minutes!"

Tunie took a shortcut through an alley. There was only one other neighborhood in all of Harbortown that Tunie knew this well—Northie, short for the Northeast End. Tunie had lived there in an apartment with her mom and dad for the first seven years of her life. There had been loads of children on their floor; the neighbors would leave their doors open, and the kids played together freely in the hallways. She could still close her eyes and navigate the Northie streets, though she hadn't been back in two years. Memories of her mom there made it too sad to return.

Tunie arrived, breathless, in front of Dringdon's Drugs. Through the window, she saw the spectacled pharmacist's assistant and felt a little lift. He was the nice one. The bell rang, announcing Tunie's entrance.

"I have . . ." Tunie counted the pennies in her hand, then gave them all to the pharmacist's assistant. "That should be enough for a few days' worth of aspirin."

"They are two for one cent. It's enough for six pills only," the assistant said regretfully. He dropped them into a little waxed paper envelope.

"Please," Tunie begged. "He's in bad shape. He has a sore throat and a fever. He really needs these to sleep."

The assistant sighed. He had a lined countenance and a gentle voice. "Everyone needs medicine, my dear. I can't just give it away, as much as I'd like to; the shop would close in a single day if I did!" Seeing Tunie's face, he softened. He glanced around and slid an extra pill into the envelope. "Oh, I'll say I dropped it," he said. "But I can't keep this up."

Tunie thanked him repeatedly, and even offered him something from the bag of day-olds, but he told her to keep them.

"Your dad will need to keep his strength up," he said. "If he has diphtheria, as I suspect, it is serious business. You need to be vaccinated so you don't contract it yourself. Aspirin might lessen his discomfort, but it won't cure him. If he isn't treated with a toxoid soon, he could develop severe complications like . . ."

Tears filled Tunie's eyes as the pharmacist stopped midsentence. A look of regret crossed his face.

"Well. You just take care of him as well as you can," he said.

"I'm trying," Tunie whispered.

CHAPTER 3

"More, more!" shouted Randall, gripping Peter's arms tightly behind his back. Pain sparked around Peter's shoulder sockets, and his ribs pressed uncomfortably against the ceramic sink. Larry, who was backed up against the wooden door, held Peter's chin in a pincer grip. The three of them hardly fit in the small lavatory. There was a disturbing trace odor of dog bombs in the close space.

Peter's eyes watered and he choked and gagged, twisting his jaw out of Larry's grip. Larry had been brushing Peter's teeth forcibly, using his father's bayberry shaving cream. The bitter flavor and chemical odor had brought Peter nearly to vomiting.

"How's it taste, smarty-pants?" Larry mocked,

waggling his furry blond eyebrows. He waved the tooth-brush back and forth before Peter's face. "Maybe just one more time. Dental hygiene is important. Open wide!"

Peter was too busy spitting out soap into the basin to respond. The corner of his mouth was bleeding from Larry's rough handling of the toothbrush. Larry startled when he caught sight of the blood, and his hand holding the toothbrush lowered.

A knock on the bathroom door made the twins jump. Randall shoved Peter away. Larry quickly fumbled the toothbrush and tube of shaving cream back into the medicine cabinet.

Peter's father called through the door. "Peter, are you in there? I have a letter for you, and Miss Cook said you never had your afternoon tea."

Peter's stepmother had gone to boarding school in England for a few years, and though she'd returned to the United States over a decade ago, she still insisted on afternoon tea.

Peter pushed past the twins and opened the door. His father stood there, slim and spectacled. He was holding a tray, upon which rested milk tea and biscuits, the news-paper, and a letter. He frowned, seeing the blood on Peter's lip as Peter tried to wipe it away.

"What's going on?" his father asked.

Once, after the twins had filled his underwear with prickly burrs, Peter had told on them. As a result, they'd all three been punished—no dessert for a week—and the twins had picked on him even more afterward.

"Nothing," Peter said. "I'm really hungry. Thank you!"

He grabbed the tray and ran past his father. Upstairs, he triple-locked the door. Peter's room was half bedroom, half workshop. On his desk, he had organized boxes of nuts and bolts, all kinds of metal pieces he'd scavenged, and various pliers and tools. On a shelf above them were machines in progress. On the cork wall, he'd pinned up articles from *Modern Mechanics* and sketches of projects he had in mind.

Peter sat down on the rug beside a small windup robot—his favorite creation of all—whom he'd named, suitably, WindUp.

He'd begun constructing WindUp a couple of weeks after his mother's funeral. Unable to sleep, he'd taken out his screwdriver and started angrily dismantling a music box his mother had sent from Switzerland, where she'd supposedly gone to recover. With brimming eyes, Peter unscrewed every tiny screw, laid bare the pieces— the neat little drum and comb, the flywheel, the spring and gears. Then he started on a clock, and next a radio. For days, his entire room was littered with parts, every surface twinkling with wires and dials and pins.

Eventually, Peter began reassembling some of the intricate cogs and circuits into something new—WindUp. The painstaking soldering and connecting gave him something to focus on besides how he was feeling. Still, the robot saw more of Peter's tears than anyone living. Peter had grown to think of WindUp as a kind of friend.

He set the tea tray on the floor beside them, first reaching for the letter with his name on it. The return address on the envelope was for Camp Contraption. Peter had written them a pleading letter, enclosing a school report card that showed his grades, and asking if they had scholarships. He tore the envelope open. Inside, there was just an advertisement, a small slip of paper with a drawing of a tent and a camper happily building some kind of scaffolding. Beneath it was printed, "There's still time! Spaces are available on a first-come, first-served basis. Full payment must be received by June 15. Don't miss out on a summer of creative fun at CAMP CONTRAPTION!"

"We have less than two weeks to come up with that money, WindUp," Peter said, holding a kerchief to his injured lip. He slumped back against the foot of his bed. "We have got to think of something."

Then his eye fell on the copy of the *Harbortown Gazette* his father had inadvertently left on the tea tray. The headline drew Peter's attention:

SEARCH CONTINUES FOR MISSING DOROTHY JAMES

Though the fair has packed up and moved on, Harbortown police continue to scour the city fairgrounds and surrounding areas for ten-year-old Dorothy James, daughter of shipping magnate Christopher James and Catherine James. Inundated with tips from citizens, police detective Dedrick Shade has followed several leads, but so far has had no luck locating the missing girl. The James family is offering a generous $1,000 reward for information leading to Dorothy's safe return. The reward has yet to be claimed.

Dorothy went missing on May 14 at the city fair's *Mummies of Ancient Egypt* exhibit, on loan from the Harbortown Natural History Museum. Her father was buying popcorn at the booth across from the exhibit. He says his daughter entered the tent, but he did not see her exit. When he followed her inside, she was nowhere to be found.

Dorothy James was last seen wearing a light blue satin party dress and matching blue ribbon headband. She has dark curly hair, brown eyes, and a heart-shaped birthmark on her left forearm. If you have any information on Dorothy's whereabouts, please contact Detective Dedrick Shade at the Harbortown Police Station on Oak Street.

"This is it, WindUp," said Peter. "I know a way into that museum! I found it on a field trip last month."

He shivered a little, just remembering it. He'd

stopped for too long at the mummy exhibit and gotten separated from his school group. Trying to find them, he ended up in a narrow passageway along the side of the building. Peter noticed a street-level window with an open latch, when all the others were locked. This was exactly the kind of thing that drove Peter crazy—he always closed cabinet doors left open, adjusted paintings hung crookedly. If five socks drying on a clothesline had toes pointing left and one pointing right, he'd flip the last so they all pointed the same direction. Seeing a single window unlocked, when every other in the row was locked, he closed the latch. Then he hurried down the hall but found it dead-ended. Peter turned a moment later and headed back the same way, only to spy the same window latch open once more. The back of his neck tingled as he glanced around the echoing hallway. He was alone. Peter figured the latch was faulty. He closed it one more time but felt disturbed enough not to look behind him as he left. He ran and found his classmates.

If he was lucky, no one had fixed that window. Despite the spooky experience he'd had, he felt a curious longing to return to the museum.

"If the police are focusing on the fairgrounds and finding nothing, I should take a look at the exhibit itself," he said to WindUp.

WindUp's blank eyes stared at Peter. Peter picked up a biscuit and munched.

"It's a place to start, anyway," he said.

The steady thuds of the twins' footfalls sounded on the stairs, followed by pounding on Peter's bedroom door.

Randall called in a menacing singsong, "Oh, Peetey! We have a new kind of pomade to try on your hair. It's better than brilliantine!"

The twins giggled.

Peter moved WindUp closer and whispered, "Don't worry, WindUp. I'll get us out of here. Promise."

CHAPTER 4

Tunie and Perch hurried down the dirt lane. The leaves rustled in the thin woods. This small stretch of forest had been preserved as part of the Harbortown Natural History Museum's property, and the semicircle of ramshackle sheds in it housed the museum's employees. Tunie's father was the janitor for the museum. He and Tunie lived in a two-room cabin that listed on its beams, half sunk into the dark earth of the woods. They'd moved in two years earlier, broke after paying her mother's medical bills. The cabin wasn't much, but Tunie knew they were lucky to have a place to live, when lots of folks were on the streets.

"Hello?" Tunie called quietly as she opened the door. Perch flew up to the rafter in the corner, his nook. Tunie had decorated it with a small homemade wind chime, some interesting twisty branches, and a crescent moon ornament she'd fashioned from a broken copper plate she'd found in an alley.

Tunie had transformed the rest of the small living area into an otherworldly space; her father had indulged Tunie and her "artist's eye," allowing her to do what she liked. Tunie had no money for paint, so she'd made her own stains, soaking walnut husks in water, and rusty nails in vinegar, and using wild blueberries and beets to make colorful dyes. She'd painted patterns on every wood panel of the place. Using a hammer and old cans, she'd fashioned glinting tin stars and hung them on threads from the rafters. There was only one small bedroom, where her father slept, so Tunie had made a kind of screen in the living room from two damaged coatracks and a printed bedsheet strung between them. Behind it was her "room": a clothing shelf made from two bricks and a board, and a mattress on the floor. She'd sewn a patchwork blanket from different scraps of fabric she'd come across, and on the walls she'd tied dried flowers she'd collected in the woods. Aside from Tunie's room, the rest of the living area was big enough for only a tiny table, one chair, and a stool near the stove. Through the doorway to her father's room, Tunie saw their elderly neighbor, Mrs. Shrubinski, carrying a jelly jar of water in her trembling hands as she approached the bed, where Tunie's father lay.

Tunie's father coughed horribly, then rasped his thanks, accepting the glass.

"How is he?" Tunie asked Mrs. Shrubinski when she tottered over.

Mrs. Shrubinski shook her head sadly and answered in her quavery voice, "Worse, I'm afraid, though he won't admit it."

Tunie opened the bag of day-old goods from Eleanor's Elegant Sweet Shoppe.

"Thanks for looking in on him. Here, take a roll for you and one for George. I'm sorry they're day-olds." George, Mrs. Shrubinski's middle-aged son, was the night watchman at the museum. Mrs. Shrubinski accepted the rolls with a shaky nod of her head.

"That's a pretty headband, dear," Mrs. Shrubinski said, touching her bony fingers to the light blue ribbon headband on Tunie's head.

Tunie smiled. "Thank you. Perch found it."

"It's very tasteful," Mrs. Shrubinski said approvingly.

After seeing their white-haired neighbor out, Tunie checked in on her father. He smiled, though he looked terrible. His skin was a bluish tone, and he had dark circles under his eyes. He'd lost his appetite and was looking more and more skeletal.

He waved a hand weakly toward the door.

"Poor Mrs. Shrub. I ought to be the one taking care of her." Then he joked, "Sweet old dame." His laugh turned into a wretched coughing fit. The cough was loud and had a strange barking sound to it. He held a handkerchief to his mouth while his whole body shook.

"Here," Tunie said, handing her father an aspirin and a glass of water. She settled in beside him, passing him a rather tough cheese scone and taking one for herself. They chewed together quietly for a few minutes. Her father made a face.

"We need to find a new bakery. The bread from this one always tastes stale," he said.

Tunie hadn't told her father that they didn't have enough money for groceries. Lots of banks—even New York's big Bank of the United States—had failed in the last few years, and their own bank was calling in debts. Tunie's father had taken out a loan to pay for her mother's medical expenses. Since then, the bank had garnished most of her dad's wages, leaving little for them to live on. Without her work for Miss Eleanor on the side, they'd be starving. As it was, they both could stand to gain a few pounds, and the aspirin wasn't helping as much as it had been. What her father desperately needed was a trip to the doctor, but they didn't have the money for it.

"We just need a little soup to soften it," Tunie said. "I'll make some tomorrow."

The room was stuffy. She stood and opened the cracked window to let in the breeze.

Her father smiled sadly at Tunie. "My little girl, so grown up already."

He started to struggle into a sitting position.

"Time for work," he said with a gasp.

"I've got it tonight, Dad," Tunie said, as she had every night for weeks. He didn't always remember.

"You need to focus on school," he argued.

"It just so happens," said Tunie, gently pushing him back into the bed and pulling up the sheet, "that summer recess began today. I can help out all summer and not miss a thing."

Her father's eyes were already fluttering closed. "All right. Maybe I will . . . get a little . . . shut-eye. . . ."

Tunie waited until he was gently snoring, and then left, whistling for Perch.

Tunie could have done the walk through the woods to the museum with her eyes closed. Some nights on her way back, it was dark enough that it felt like she was doing just that. Now the golden setting sun made the tree branches look as if they were aflame.

Out of the woods, she crossed the small, grassy field to the side entrance of the museum and used one of the iron keys to get in the door.

The door opened to a stairwell. She heard a familiar voice calling down from the floor above.

"That you, Tunie?" said her neighbor, the night watchman.

"Hello, George. It's me," said Tunie. "Just stepping in for my dad again."

George's affable face appeared at the railing on the floor above. He smiled, showing crooked teeth.

"I'm sorry your dad's not better, but I'm glad to see you," he said.

"Thanks, George," said Tunie warmly. George was as sweet and sympathetic as his mother. Tunie wondered what he'd do if he ever did encounter a burglar in the museum—invite him over for dinner, probably.

George cleared his throat. "The museum manager said he'd be coming by later tonight, something about checking on a third-floor installation. I'll try to keep him upstairs, but just wanted to let you know."

"Gotcha. Thanks for the warning."

"Sure thing."

The museum manager, Mr. Narfgau, had caught Tunie cleaning once and was terribly angry about it. He said he wasn't paying for child labor, he'd hired a professional, and he'd give her dad the boot if he found out Tunie was doing his work again.

Tunie went about her business, filling the bucket with Lin-X and warm water, and hauling it down the hall. She opened the door to the Ancient Egypt exhibit.

Of all the exhibits in the museum, Tunie liked this one best. She felt a kind of energy about the space, the same strange, humming sensation she'd experienced when she first spied Perch hanging from a bare branch in her mother's graveyard.

On that wet day, by herself among the gloomy tombstones, Tunie had felt unafraid. She noticed the bat clinging to a damp tree near her mother's grave. She knew bats weren't usually awake in the afternoon, as this one was. He watched her with large, almost child-like eyes. Tunie's skin was vibrating all over, like a tuning fork. She placed all but one of the wildflowers she'd brought on her mother's grave. She held out the remaining single bloom to the bat. He swooped down, grabbed the flower, and perched on Tunie's satchel. Tunie lifted her bag with the bat atop it so she could see the little animal eye to eye.

"Hello. I like the looks of you. What should I call you?" Tunie said. She thought for a moment. "How about . . . Perch?"

The bat clutched the flower. He swayed a little from left to right, almost like he was dancing. His head was round and furry. It seemed he ought to go home with her, and he did.

Now Perch flew into the Ancient Egypt exhibit and hung from a statue's carved scythe. Tunie started mopping, feeling the familiar prickling on her skin.

The exhibit was belowground, a long, boxlike room that was perpetually shadowy, even during the day. The air inside was cool. It was like breathing in a cavern, and it always smelled of a peculiar, smoky incense. In the center of the room were three stone sarcophagi, one of which was heartbreakingly small. Tunie could have fit inside.

The walls were lined with shelves of statuary depicting various Egyptian gods, many with animal heads, and pieces of stone with carved writing taken from temples. Brass plaques explained the history of each item. There were also displays of canopic jars and pottery, and glass cases containing ancient daggers and weapons. Sound echoed a bit in this chamber; more than once Tunie had heard people say the place was ghostly. It was difficult to identify its appeal, but Tunie felt drawn to the exhibit far more than any other.

This night, however, after swabbing the tile floor for a few moments, Tunie paused. She had the unnerving feeling someone was watching.

"Perch?" she called. Tunie realized the lights had been on when she came into the room. Usually she had to turn them on herself. She held still, listening. Was that the sound of someone breathing?

"Perch!" Tunie shouted. A cough made her whirl in fright, and she tripped over the feet of a young boy who was tucked up and hiding behind a canopic jar. Tunie staggered, barely keeping her balance. Then she brandished her mop, threatening the intruder with its soggy end.

"Who are you? How did you get in here?" she demanded.

The boy raised both hands as if Tunie held a pistol, not a mop. His brown eyes were wide.

"I'm Peter. Last time I was here, I found a window with a busted latch. I was just . . . I was only looking around, I swear! I wasn't going to take anything," he said.

Perch flew in and whapped his black, rubbery wings around the boy's face a few times, until Peter ducked down with his arms over his head. Perch landed on Tunie's shoulder and gave his best menacing hiss, eyeing the intruder.

Tunie lowered the mop a bit. The boy looked about her age, nine or ten, and he spoke politely. His brown hair was trimmed, and his kneesocks and knickers were fairly neat, if not fancy. He didn't look like a vagrant.

Tunie straightened her back, feeling slightly more courageous. "My bat bites, and I know the night watchman. He can hear me, you know."

Peter dropped his hands. "Please, don't tell on me."

"The museum's closed. What are you doing here?" Tunie frowned. "Tell me the truth straightaway, or I'm shouting for help."

The boy sighed. "I'm looking for clues. A girl went missing from this exhibit at the fair. I figured if the coppers are still searching the fairgrounds, I'd look over the exhibit and maybe find something that could help them."

Tunie lowered the mophead to the floor. She understood. "You want the reward."

"Yes." The boy looked a little embarrassed. "But I'd like to help the girl, too."

Tunie gestured at the exhibit. "The police already sifted through everything, you know, as did every single person who read about the kidnapping. What makes you think you could do something they can't?"

The boy bent down to pick up a canvas knapsack from the floor. He seemed less afraid now. He had freckles and a small nose. Tunie thought his face was friendly.

"I'm . . ." The boy's cheeks went pink. "I'm pretty smart, I guess. I mean at problem solving, particularly. And building things."

"Uh-huh," Tunie said, doubtful.

"Look, I'll show you," Peter said. He opened his knapsack and took out a small mechanical robot. He patted the top of the robot, and it made a sweet sound like a music box note.

Perch narrowed his eyes at the strange creature. Tunie raised an eyebrow. "You're going to use your toy?"

Realizing the robot wasn't alive, Perch made a soft snickering sound.

"I built this. His name is WindUp. Say hi, WindUp," Peter said. He turned a key on WindUp's back. The robot waved jerkily, then took a bow.

Tunie had to smile. "That's cute as a bug's ear. You really made him?"

"I sure did. I found—"

A bang sounded from an adjacent room. Tunie startled and, turning, saw that the door on the far wall was ajar.

She eyed the door. "That's the employee kitchen, but George never uses it, not ever."

Tunie and Peter exchanged a fearful glance. Peter stuffed WindUp back into his bag, and together they tiptoed past a sarcophagus and a glass display case of handmade bowls until they reached the open door. Tunie felt that humming sensation again, more forcefully than before.

They peered into the kitchen. There, rifling through the cupboards, was a diminutive figure, bound head to toe in filthy bandages. It moved stiffly, one wrapped hand holding a mug with a picture of a red cardinal on it.

The thing turned its bandaged face toward them. Suddenly Tunie recognized it. She'd seen the child's corpse lying still in its sarcophagus many times. A strip of linen, resting where its eyebrows might have been, lifted. Beneath gleamed two enormous golden eyes.

"Hullo!" the mummy said delightedly. Two linen strips smiled, as if they were lips. He gestured to the kettle.

"Tea?"

Tunie and Peter and Perch screamed.

CHAPTER 5

The children kept shrieking with terror as the mummy took a sip from his mug. Amber liquid dripped through his partially exposed rib cage and down a few loose bandages into puddles on the floor.

"I'm parched," said the mummy in a scratchy voice.

Suddenly they heard a man's voice and running footsteps.

Tunie managed to stop screaming and turned, expecting to see George looking goofy in his oversized uniform. Instead, bald Mr. Narfgau, the museum manager, stood in the doorway, glaring.

"You again!" he said, narrowing his eyes at Tunie. "What did I tell you? Now you're sneaking your friends in here?" He waved a hand at Peter. He didn't even glance at the mummy. The mummy edged closer and closer. Tunie stood still, petrified.

Mr. Narfgau was turning a shade of strawberry. He raised his voice. "I knew that night watchman was up to something! He was trying to keep me upstairs—he knew you were down here, didn't he?"

"Sir," said Peter. "We saw this mummy and . . ."

He stopped. The mummy had wiggled in between Tunie and Peter, slinging one bony arm around each of their shoulders. Tunie was too terrified to move. Mr. Narfgau, who had been glaring at the two of them, stopped and glanced around the kitchen, confused. He touched his thick mustache and then took a handkerchief out of his breast pocket to wipe his shiny scalp.

"Now, what was I doing down here?" he muttered to himself.

"I can explain—" Tunie said, but the mummy interrupted.

"Shhh," he said. His breath smelled like smoky incense. Tunie hushed.

Mr. Narfgau sighed. He continued to look puzzled, but when he spoke, he sounded calmer.

"Hmm. I must have been getting some water for myself and that nice George. That's it," he said. He pottered around for a moment. He filled two glasses with water and then slowly walked out.

"Strange . . . ," he said. "I must be really tired."

It was as if Mr. Narfgau could no longer see them; he looked directly at them but seemed to register nothing.

They watched him walk across the floor and exit through the door to the exhibit.

Tunie had to take several deep breaths before she could talk.

"H-how did you do that?" she asked the mummy.

The mummy lowered his skinny arms and stepped back.

"I suppose it was the magic of my curse. I wasn't sure it would work, really," he said.

"Well, that was aces. Thanks. I'm Tunie, and this is my bat, Perch," she said in a trembling voice. "Nice to meet you, Parched."

The mummy chuckled merrily.

Peter said, "That isn't what he meant when he said he was parched. 'Parched' means 'thirsty.'"

Tunie flushed. "Oh, right."

"I'm Peter," he said to the mummy. He'd been clenching his knapsack tightly in both hands, but now he loosened his grip and slung it over his shoulder.

The mummy bowed. "I'm Horus. It is my great pleasure to meet you."

Tunie's fear began to dissipate. The mummy wasn't much bigger than they were, and seemed pretty fragile. The linen strips around his stomach had loosened, giving him a rather adorable potbellied look.

Horus cleared his throat. "You can repay me, you know. I'm dying for some company—no pun intended. Please join me for some tea."

Tunie carefully set aside her mop. She hadn't noticed

she was still clutching it. "All right. Thanks again. Mr. Narfgau's the big boss around here; he would have fired my father for sure."

"I'm glad I could help!" Horus said. "Please, sit down. This is already the best luck I've had in a millennium."

Tunie pulled out a chair, and so did Peter.

In possibly the oddest tea party ever arranged, Peter, Tunie, Perch, and Horus the mummy sat elbow to elbow around the undersized table. They passed a packet of stale Hydrox cookies with the teapot. Tunie noticed that Horus was holding something in his hand. When he set it down to lift the teapot, she saw what it was—a smooth rock with a worn, carved symbol. She recognized it from a display in the exhibit that was near Horus's sarcophagus—it was a projectile for an ancient sling weapon. Tunie poured a small saucer of cream for Perch. She hoped they wouldn't get in trouble for taking these things, but Horus said they were provided by the museum for its employees and no one had ever minded when he'd helped himself—or perhaps the curse kept them from noticing; he wasn't sure.

Tunie sipped her tea and carefully examined the mummy. "Why do you look like a kid but talk like a British grandpa? Won't that tea make your bandages all soggy? What curse? And I thought you were an unknown mummy."

Horus managed to look intensely pleased. Instead of covering his face, the bandages somehow seemed to move like facial muscles, and the weird glow of his eyes was surprisingly warm. He smiled as he ticked off responses to Tunie's questions on his fingers.

"One: I died when I was only ten. I spent more than a century in a British museum and learned to speak English from the stuffy curator there, developing this accent and an incredible thirst for tea, which, two, doesn't do a thing to me. The enchantment of my curse must keep it from damaging me so I can continue to suffer an eternity of regret. And lastly: just because the archaeologists who dug me up didn't know me doesn't mean I'm not Horus, the lesser-known little brother of pharaoh Taharqa. I never lived out my childhood, but I've been around for ages."

Tunie let out a breath. "So now you're an ancient . . . kid mummy . . . who talks like a tweedy professor."

"Murder, that's a story," said Peter. His eyes were wide. He studied the mummy with interest.

Horus propped his chin on one bandaged hand and wistfully watched Perch lap up the cream. "I've often wished for a familiar, someone to keep me company. Eternity, as you might imagine, is an awfully long time."

Peter said with a tone of slight skepticism, "So you are animated by *magic*? How did it happen?"

Horus gave a dry cough. "I'll try to keep it short. Let's see, this was about 701 BC or thereabouts. Our kingdom was in conflict with Assyria. My older brother wasn't pharaoh yet, but he was a commander at the time. He fought proudly, and I . . . didn't. I did more . . ." He paused, as if uncertain about saying it aloud. Then he said all at once, "Uh, destroying our enemies' belongings. Looting. All right, robbing, really."

Tunie's uneasiness at this personal history must have shown on her face.

Horus leaned forward and rushed to say, "Oh, believe me, I wish I could take it all back! I've had ages to learn how horrible I was. At any rate, in one home as I was, uh, smashing a set of figurines—statues depicting Nephthys, protector of the dead—an old grandmother cursed me to 'an eternity of regret in the house of death' for my 'destructive nature.' A heavy figurine fell on my head and killed me, right then, so I died days after my tenth birthday. She fumbled the words a bit, so I'm not stuck in a tomb anymore, now that I've been unearthed. I can move, but only at night. I have found, though, that I cannot leave the rooms of the exhibit in which I am kept. Yet traveling between museums seems to work, and this small kitchen is accessible. I'd bet something about the curse drew you to me, too, since you can see me when most can't." Horus made a rustling noise as he shrugged. "Curses. Who understands them?"

"I'd never believe it if I weren't sitting here, talking to you." Peter sounded bewildered. He absentmindedly handed his cookie over to Tunie. She accepted it with a smile.

"One thing I don't get," Tunie said, "is why I can see

you tonight. I've cleaned this place a bunch of times. Why couldn't I see you before?"

Horus glanced back and forth from Tunie to Peter and raised his palms. "Perhaps you both had to be here in order for me to be revealed?"

Tunie considered this. "Does everything you touch turn invisible to others, the way Mr. Narfgau couldn't see us when you put your arms around us?"

"Not exactly," Horus said. "People don't see things related to me. For example"—he hefted the rock in his hand—"every day, I smash a display case to take out this rock. Did you notice the broken glass?" he asked Tunie.

Tunie shook her head, eyes wide.

Horus continued. "Neither did anyone at the British Museum when this exhibit was there. If I stand in someone's path, he or she will usually walk around me. People don't sense me in any way, even if they bump into me. I've tried leaping on people's backs, and they don't stumble or even seem to feel it. When I make a mess, no one notices. Sometimes, if I'm doing something directly in front of a person, he or she will grow confused and turn away, like your Mr. Narfgau. I've never turned anyone invisible before, but then, no one else has interacted with me the way you did tonight."

Peter was listening intently to Horus.

"It makes sense, if the curse keeps people from seeing things that would draw attention to you," Peter said. "If a person saw us interacting with something invisible, that would be strange and attract interest. It could be the curse sort of . . . clouded us in front of Mr. Narfgau because of that."

Horus agreed. "Precisely. Of course, I haven't had much opportunity to test the curse. Very few people visit the exhibit after hours—usually only the cleaning crew, or a night watchman, or a museum curator. For the most part, I am on my own."

Peter asked Horus, "What happens if you try to leave the room?"

Horus looked uncomfortable. "It is . . . terribly unpleasant. It feels a bit like, uh, drowning. Burning lungs. Also like walking on coals and being attacked by voracious fire ants and stinging bees and venomous snakes. Not my favorite thing to do," he said. "Enough about me. I know about me. Let's talk about you all for a moment. I can help you, you know—*if* you do some things for me."

Tunie swallowed the last of Peter's cookie. "Help us with what?"

Horus said, "You're interested in finding the girl who was kidnapped from my exhibit at the fair, aren't you?"

Peter leaned over the table toward Horus.

"Were you there?" Peter asked.

The mummy made a face. "Oh, yes. Distasteful situation. I'll tell you what I know, if you make me a promise."

"What's that?" Tunie said with suspicion.

Horus blinked his luminous eyes. "Promise me you'll come back. You're the only people who have been able to interact with me since a toddler greeted me with a rag doll once, in England. That must have been a hundred years ago. Promise you'll come back—and bring me something to read, to pass the time."

Tunie looked over the mummy. He was stained a bit brown and gray with age, and the bones where they showed through his wraps were disturbing, but for all that—and his former thieving ways—he seemed . . . polite, at least.

"I'll bring you some library books, Horus," she said.

Peter looked thoughtful. "My father reads the paper, too. I can bring some of those."

"Excellent! Someone left one in here once. It named all kinds of wonders—moving pictures, motorcars, bubble gum!" The mummy clapped his hands. "I want to know more about everything. Oh, and I especially liked the comics!"

"Great. I'll bring as many as I can. Now, please," Peter said fervently, "tell us! What do you know about Dorothy James's kidnapping?"

CHAPTER 6

Peter tried to sit still, but he felt keyed up, knowing the mummy had been at the scene of the crime. An undead eyewitness! This was something the coppers definitely hadn't discovered!

The mummy took a sip of tea and began. "They were unsavory fellows, much like my grave-robber comrades. Not to be trusted, of course, but they knew how to have fun! Well, at least, they did at first. . . . Where was I? Oh, yes. There were two kidnappers. One had a terrifically nasal voice and smelled of hickory woodsmoke. He came quite near my sarcophagus, and though I couldn't see his face, I distinctly heard him say he had to be back at Franklin Street by midnight."

Peter was breathless with elation. "This is great! Inside information! What about the accomplice?"

Horus appeared pleased by Peter's exuberance. "The other was also a man, but his voice was low and muffled. I heard the girl shriek from his direction, and then it sounded like he was covering her mouth." The mummy looked thoughtful for a moment. "There was something else. He made a strange tapping sound when he walked."

"That's keen! I know where Franklin Street is," Tunie said delightedly. "All we have to do is find the man with the nasal voice!"

Peter frowned. "Wait a minute. This is *my* investigation. I need that dough."

He touched the injured corner of his mouth, remembering what he had to escape. "I'm going to have every bone in my body broken this summer if I can't get out of town."

Tunie blinked. "I need the money, too. My dad is sick and we can't afford a doctor."

Peter stared at Tunie for a moment. He liked her. He knew from experience, though, that most people couldn't get away from him fast enough once the twins appeared, and his stepbrothers were almost impossible to avoid. What if, during their research into this kidnapping, she decided she didn't want to be near Peter? What was to keep her from using the information they'd gathered together, going after the reward on her own, and taking all the money?

"Once I get it, I'll share some with you, but I have to get that reward myself. It was nice to meet you, Horus," he said, standing. "Thanks for the information. I'm going to work on the case now. I promise I'll bring you something to read."

"Wait! You're leaving?" Tunie sounded stunned.

"Sorry, Tunie. I gotta get started tonight." Peter took his mug to the sink. The disappointment on her face made him feel ashamed. In his friendliest voice, he said, "I'll be seeing you, okay?"

Tunie simply kept looking at him with wide eyes and open mouth. Feeling decidedly uncomfortable, Peter hurried out of the room.

CHAPTER 7

"What a curve," Tunie said, disappointed. "I thought we were going to be a team—the Harbortown Investigators or Horus and Company. Something like that."

Horus looked thoughtful. "He did rush off, didn't he? I wonder why he's set on doing this himself. He must have some reason."

Perch squeaked.

"I know," Tunie said. "I'd better get around to cleaning the rest of this place. What can he do with a head start at night, anyway? Thanks for the lowdown, Horus. And the tea."

With a crinkle, Horus rose from his chair. "I'll help you clean, if you like. I've been bored for centuries."

Alone with the little mummy, Tunie was beginning to

feel spooked. She thought about the curse drawing her and Peter here like some unseen supernatural current, and the statue of Nephthys, protector of the dead, that Horus had broken. Could this Nephthys be watching them? She shivered.

"Uh, I'm about done here. I need to get to the other exhibits. Thanks, though."

The mummy slumped, looking even smaller. He scraped the floor with one bandaged foot. "I wish I could go with you! I'd give anything to see even one more floor of this place."

He gestured to the floor overhead, linen strips flapping around his hands. Tunie felt sympathetic suddenly. How unspeakably boring it would be, sitting in this exhibit night after night, all alone! She might not want to spend too much time rubbing elbows with a curse, but she did pity Horus. An eternity was a long jail sentence. Everyone had regrets. Tunie winced, remembering the time she and her dad had a bad stretch of days with no food. Tunie had snuck into Eleanor's Elegant Sweet Shoppe when she knew the baker would be taking her lunch break. She'd stolen a warm loaf of bread straight off the cooling rack and darted out. Nobody had ever mentioned it to her. Tunie didn't know if anyone had even noticed the missing loaf. Every time she spied that cooling rack, however, she felt ashamed.

Tunie turned to the mummy and said, "I'll swing by with some library books tomorrow. We can stash them in one of the kitchen cabinets."

Horus's yellow eyes grew wet. He clasped his hands together in front of his chest. His voice trembled with eagerness. "That would be a miracle!"

Tunie patted the dry bindings on Horus's hand.

"I'll be back as soon as I can," she promised.

She grabbed her mop and headed for the door. Looking back, she watched Horus staring after her with his weirdly illuminated eyes. Why couldn't she shake this creepy feeling that he was hiding something?

CHAPTER 8

After Peter and Tunie left, Horus was filled with excited energy. He'd been seen! He'd interacted with the living!

"I do hope I came across as likable," he said, climbing on top of the table in the small staff kitchen, his sling stone in hand. He hadn't been lying about wanting a familiar; he'd been alone for so long he'd developed the habit of speaking aloud to himself.

"If they like me, they might come back! Of course they'll come back. They said they would."

Swinging his arms, Horus jumped down with a satisfying thump. Then he stepped on a chair and climbed up on the table again.

"I'll start small, yes. Just books at first. Then a pen! Yes. Yes, yes, I need a pen. Then—what else? Oh, a musical instrument! Several! Art supplies! Games of some kind!"

He jumped down again, shaking the furniture slightly, then immediately climbed back up.

Table jumping was one of the many pastimes Horus had taken to over the decades. He'd done everything he could think of to amuse himself. He'd built gigantic dioramas of Egyptian cities out of cups and sugar packets. He'd used water and newspaper to make a kind of paste, and created paper-paste sculptures of sphinxes and rams and the sun god, Ra. Talking to Tunie and Peter, he'd glossed over the true horror of his afterlife. For example, he'd spent his first century motionless in the pitch-black dark of a tomb. He could see nothing. He could not get up and walk about. There was nothing to do during his animate hours but lie in the dark and cry and shout and, finally, scream. He had screamed for what seemed like forever. Then, mercifully, he'd gone into a kind of fuzzy hibernation for centuries, until some archaeologists had dug him up.

That night decades ago, when he'd initially woken in the British Museum and could escape the prison of his sarcophagus, he'd been filled with wicked glee. The very first evening, he'd trashed the exhibit, smashing jars and vases and centuries-old carvings, ripping paintings off walls, tearing everything apart.

"Who's cursed now?!" he'd shouted, laughing maniacally at the pure devastation.

Then, as the clock had ticked toward the early hours of the morning, everything had been restored to order in a blink, and he had once again been frozen in his sarcophagus.

He'd gone on and ruined the exhibit, night after night, raging against his curse, until one day the desire to break things simply dissipated.

After that, he learned that anything he took from people in the exhibit returned to its place as soon as he was back in his sarcophagus. Horus attempted to steal things—he pulled a trailing scarf from a night watchman's neck, a thermos from a janitor's bag. The owners never seemed aware they were missing anything, but the items vanished from Horus's hands with the sunrise. Only items truly forgotten by their owners or purposefully left behind in the exhibit remained.

Eventually, he'd taken the time to look around the exhibit. He read the brass plaques on various cases and found out what had happened to his people. He learned that his older brother, Taharqa, whom he'd envied, had eventually become pharaoh, and had reigned during what was considered a renaissance period. He'd even built new temples and a great pyramid. In the end, however, he had lost to Esarhaddon, the Assyrian king, and had to flee. His enemy took away Taharqa's children and queen. Instead of feeling any kind of satisfaction at this revelation, Horus fell to the floor. He hunched, his back pressing against a case of crumbling rock art, and wept for his proud brother's defeat. Then, in another case, Horus discovered a marvel: the very sling stone his brother had once given to him as a present, carved with a symbol of Taharqa's own design. Horus shattered the case and pulled out the rock. It was all he had of the family he'd lost. He gripped it as if it were his brother's hand.

After this period, there was a long stretch during which Horus hoarded things people dropped in the exhibit— candy wrappers, calling cards, informational pamphlets about the museum, pencil stubs, bobby pins, string.

He'd lied to Tunie and Peter about the girl who'd greeted him with a rag doll back in England. It was a lie of omission; there was more to the story, but he was ashamed of it. One night, there had been a charity event in the museum—a special showcase with food and drink—to help raise money for impoverished children. It was shockingly well attended. Horus's exhibit was crowded, wall-to-wall with people. The girl with the rag doll also had a set of colored pencils. She had wandered away from her parents, and Horus discovered her sobbing in the corner.

"I can't find my mum!" she cried, looking right at him.

She could see him! Instead of wanting to help the lost little girl, however, Horus was overcome with longing for her colored pencils. For ages, he'd yearned for someone to leave behind just such a thing, and now here they were, within reach! The desire for them was so strong, he didn't pause to appreciate the marvel of the human contact that was taking place, until it was too late. He never would learn how she had seen him.

"Give me your pencils," Horus said, "and I'll take you to your parents."

The girl clutched the pencils to her chest and shrieked. "Noooo!"

Horus could hear a man and a woman calling, "Clara? Clara?"

"I'll help you find them. Just give the pencils to me!"

"They're mine!"

"Give them to me!"

The girl screamed, and people around her began to stare. Horus managed to wrest the colored pencils from her damp hands and dash off with them, leaving her wailing. Soon she and the other guests departed. In a kind of frenzy, he drew all over the walls, on every blank space. He furiously sketched everything he could remember from his life—the crocodiles and fish and ibises with curved beaks he'd seen when he visited the river Nile, the clouds making their easy travels across the sky. He drew fig trees and cattle, antelopes and hippopotamuses, and every face and temple he could recall. At the end of the evening, however, the stolen colored pencils vanished with the rising sun. Horus wept for days, not only for the loss of those most precious art supplies and the home he'd never know again, but for his own behavior. He'd had the opportunity to help a lost little girl and what had he done? He was a monster.

Horus ceased jumping from the kitchen table and stopped to think on a chair.

Here, once again, he'd had the opportunity to help others, and what had he done? Well, he *had* helped them, Horus told himself. He'd given them useful information that could in turn save a kidnapped child! Surely, that was good. But deep down, Horus knew he'd done it first and foremost out of greed: he'd helped them because he wanted something from them. This avaricious part of himself had always gotten him into trouble, Horus thought with a sigh. Millennia later, and he still could be a better person.

CHAPTER 9

The next day, as the Harbortown trolley rattled through the early-morning mist, Peter held his knapsack to his chest and thought about the night before. If he'd slept at all, he would have thought meeting Horus was a dream. It seemed surreal, compared with this moment. The streetcar was filled mostly with women and men presumably going to work, the women in knit day suits, the men in subdued coats and flat hats and trousers. He was heading to Franklin Street to follow up on Horus's clue from the night before and feeling decidedly guilty.

I certainly will share the reward with Tunie, and Horus, too, if I can find a way, Peter thought, to make himself feel better. Tunie had seemed nice, but what if she got the reward? Would she really share it with him? Peter couldn't take the chance. He gently placed a hand on his ribs where they still ached from Randall shoving him against the hard sink. He had to get away from his stepbrothers. It wasn't just that they hurt him; it was how they made him feel—helpless, weak, and ashamed somehow. He clenched the bag in his hands harder, just thinking about it. Going to the camp wouldn't be a simple escape, either; it would be something he'd achieved himself, proof that he could do anything if he tried hard enough.

As the trolley approached Franklin Street, Peter pulled the string, ringing the brass bell up front and signaling the driver to stop.

On the relatively empty street, Peter donned the headpiece he'd spent the entire night creating. It was a metal headband affixed to two ear trumpets, like weird, twisty tin rabbit's ears. He'd designed his own with modifications from pictures of ones Beethoven had used. They were like funnels, with a wider end to collect sound waves and a smaller end to direct the waves to the ears.

"Time to try them out, WindUp," Peter said over his shoulder to the robot, who was peeking out from the back of his knapsack.

"Lookin' for space aliens, kid? Or are you one yourself?" Two men in boaters and linen suits laughed together as they passed Peter on the street. Their voices were loud in his ears, and Peter flinched. Still, he was pleased—the ear trumpets worked amazingly well. He could hear the creak of shutters as someone opened a window over a shop.

A woman carrying a basket of bread passed by and

smiled at Peter. "Bit early for a costume party, isn't it, hon?"

Peter only shrugged, listening for any voice that was particularly nasal, as Horus had mentioned. None yet. Peter had been to this part of town only a few times; it was near the wharf, and there was a whole section of high-crime neighborhoods farther south. This stretch, however, was a fairly viable commercial neighborhood, with two- and three-story buildings that had shops on the ground-level floors and residences above. Most of the shops weren't open yet. Here and there, homeless people lay across the sidewalks, sleeping. There weren't as many as there had been a couple of years ago, but Peter's father said the country was still recovering from the Great Depression.

He was too early. There weren't many people around to investigate. Peter decided to sit on a bench with WindUp, read an old *Weird Tales* comic, and eat the breakfast he'd packed, until the day's hubbub was really under way. He kept his headpiece on, just in case, but soon became absorbed in the comic. After a while, a traffic cop's shrill whistle reverberated in his ears. He looked up, startled to see that the morning bustle had begun in earnest when he wasn't paying attention.

Peter started making his way up the busy sidewalk, eavesdropping on conversations between shopkeepers:

"That display of pumps is looking snazzy, Lila."

"I hope the customers think so!"

"Good morning!" Peter said to the people who were walking alone beneath the scalloped awnings of the ice-cream parlor and café, and to the man in the straw panama hat lingering outside the radio repair shop. Most of them returned the greeting, surprised at this odd-looking but friendly child, and he listened to their voices to hear if they were nasal. No luck.

Then, walking into a crowd, Peter realized his mistake.

When he'd passed people one at a time, the listening device had worked well, but in a group the din of voices was overwhelming, the cacophony painful and impossible to parse. He cringed at the earsplitting clamor. He'd never be able to pick out a nasally voice from this ruckus! Peter turned and tried to get away from the clutch of people. He bumped into someone and looked up. There, waiting outside a woman's dress shop, were Larry and Randall, looking dully displeased, their wet yellow hair neatly combed across their foreheads. He'd forgotten that their mother was dragging the twins around today to buy new summer clothes, as they'd outgrown last year's. Larry's eyes lit upon Peter, and he smiled.

Peter spun around, ready to run, but a flock of sun-bonneted old ladies outside a tea shop blocked his path.

Randall charged forward and grabbed Peter by one arm, dragging him into a narrow alley between two buildings.

Larry flicked his fingers against one of Peter's ear horns.

"What do we have here?" Larry asked in his taunting voice. Peter grimaced at the volume.

Larry continued gibing.

"I thought it was our *genius* stepbrother, but now I see it's a little rabbit! Let's hang this rabbit upside down, Randall," he ordered.

Randall knocked Peter down onto the gritty, puddled ground and then jerked him up so he was dangling from his ankles.

Here we go again, Peter thought dismally.

CHAPTER 10

The clang of a metal pot woke Tunie. Her eyes stung, but she pulled aside the curtain that was the wall of her room anyhow.

"Dad? What time is it?" she asked, yawning.

Her father was rifling through the cabinets. "The cupboards are bare! Why don't you take some money from the emergency jar and get us some breakfast?" He seemed unfocused, looking around with watery eyes.

Tunie leaped to her feet, hurrying to hide the empty, cobweb-covered emergency fund jar.

"Have a pastry, Dad," she said.

He took a bite of a two-day-old strawberry Danish and chewed without pleasure. "Eh, this bakery. These always taste stale," he said. He finished it nevertheless, but when he stood for a glass of water, he crumpled against the sink.

Tunie rushed to his side and helped him to his chair by the window. The morning was warm, but he shivered anyway, and Tunie covered his legs with a worn blanket. She saw that his legs were wasting away, hardly thicker than the spindly legs of the chair now.

"You need to see a doctor, Dad," she said tearfully. "Let's just go to the physician's office. Please! They couldn't turn you away, not if they saw how sick you are."

But her father was firm. "No. We won't go begging." He coughed with a horrible barking sound into his handkerchief and leaned his head back, closing his eyes. "I just need a little rest, that's all. And maybe some soup later."

Tunie watched as her father fell back asleep, his breath rattling in his chest. Then, with renewed determination, she kissed his gaunt cheek and whistled for Perch. She placed her blue headband on her head firmly, as if donning armor.

"Come on, Perch," she said, grabbing a bucket and sponge from beside the sink. "We have a kidnapping to solve."

Once on Franklin Street, Tunie explained her plan to Perch. "I'm going to wash windows, to give me an excuse for staying on this street all day. I'll keep an eye out for anybody with a cane—I think that might be the tapping sound Horus heard when one of them walked. You fly up over the people here, see if you spy anybody with a cane. Got it?"

The bat seemed to salute Tunie with one tiny claw and flapped away, up over the rooftops.

Tunie started washing the windows of a butcher shop with a sign that read PEPPERMAN'S PRIME CUTS. A heavyset man in an apron came out.

He gave Tunie a disgruntled look. "I didn't ask anyone to clean my windows."

Tunie feigned surprise. "Isn't this the address?" She pretended to peer at the number on the shop's door. "Oops." She shrugged. "I might as well finish the job. Don't worry—I'll do it for free. The guy I work for will pay me, s'long as I get to the right one eventually."

She shot him her most winning grin.

The butcher softened. "That's all right, then. Come see me when you're done for the day and heading home. I might have something for you."

Tunie smiled. "I sure will. Thank you, sir," she said, and continued scrubbing the cloudy glass—which really did need a cleaning. There was an empty fruit crate outside the shop, and Tunie stood on it, stretching to reach the top of the pane. The job took much longer than Tunie had anticipated, and the only person she saw with a cane was a hunched old woman moving at a tortoise crawl. She could hardly be a kidnapper.

The sun was hot on the back of Tunie's neck, her fingers were pruning, and she was beginning to doubt her entire plan. At this rate, it'd take her a week to make it up and down the street. And what if the tapping hadn't been a cane? What if the sound had been something else entirely? Her spirits plummeted.

Just as she finished the window, Tunie heard voices around the corner. She peered down the alley, and to her surprise, there was Peter! He had something crazy on his head and was being shaken, upside down, by two bigger kids.

"What's a little rabbit afraid of?" the leaner one of the bullies jeered. "A fox? A fox's pointy fangs?" He jabbed at Peter's midsection with a stick.

"Ouch!" Peter said in a strained voice. His face was turning an alarming purple red. "What, do you just carry sharp sticks around in case you need to torture somebody?"

Tunie whistled for Perch and then stepped into the shadowy alley.

"Two against one?" she said loudly. "And bigger to boot. You are some kind of cowardly bullies."

The larger boy holding Peter's ankles stared at Tunie. "Who are you?"

Tunie caught sight of Perch flying overhead. She lifted her chin toward the one holding Peter and saw Perch begin his dive.

She smiled. "I'm the one who's going to even these odds."

In one rapid move, she sloshed water from her bucket into the face of the angular twin with the stick. The soapy water stung his eyes.

"Argh!" the boy shouted, bending over, with his hands covering his eyes.

There was a muffled grunt as Peter dropped to the ground. The twin who'd been holding him began running in great, lumbering circles and flailing his arms. He shrieked in a high-pitched voice.

"A bat! It's a vampire bat! Help! It's attacking me! Aaaaargh!"

Perch was clearly enjoying himself, flapping with gusto around the boy's face.

Peter scrambled to his feet, and he and Tunie took off, with Perch soon flying behind them.

They ran up the road until they were sure the twins weren't following them, and stopped to catch their breath on the street corner.

Tunie looked with concern at Peter. There was a spot of blood seeping through his shirt where one of the boys had poked him.

"Those two are plenty rugged. I'm guessing they're the ones you want to get away from this summer?" Tunie said.

"Yeah," said Peter glumly. "They're my new step-brothers."

"That's unlucky."

"I can avoid them most of the time, and when my dad's in the room, they won't touch me. He's leaving, though, for the summer, and now that school's out . . . I can't fend them off forever. If I had enough money, I'd go to camp to get away." He sighed and started fiddling with one bent ear of his strange helmet. "Thanks for helping me out. Most folks aren't interested in tangling with the twins." He looked up to meet Tunie's eyes. "I'm sorry I ran off last night. I really am planning to share the reward with you."

"I guess you're out of practice trusting people. I'm beginning to see why." Tunie gave him a wry smile. "I'm on the lookout for someone with a cane—I figure that's the tapping sound Horus mentioned."

"That's a good theory," Peter said.

Tunie shrugged. "Actually, I'm not having much luck. So far the only person with a cane was a frail old lady just barely on this side of heaven."

Peter looked dolefully at his headpiece. "This device was supposed to help me find the man with the nasal voice, but in these crowds it's useless. So far I've got nothing."

"Look. This street is really long," Tunie said. She waved her hand from one side to the other. "It'll take forever to comb over it alone, and by then it might be too late. Let's work together. You and I can split the money, fifty-fifty, and find some way to share with Horus, too. I promise I won't let you down."

Peter shook Tunie's hand. "It's a deal. I'm not sure either one of us is going about this the right way, though. No offense. I just . . . I don't see how we'll ever find these guys."

Tunie drooped. Perch fluttered down and landed on her shoulder, emitting a series of unhappy squeaks.

Peter observed the bat. "You know, Horus is extraordinary, but your bat is also extremely abnormal. If you'd asked me last week whether such bizarre things existed, I would have laughed. I still can't quite accept it."

"Most people couldn't. I keep thinking maybe last night didn't happen."

"Me too," Peter said. "But since we're both here talking about a mummy we met, I guess it did."

"We haven't been able to use what he told us, though," Tunie said. She dropped her sponge into the soapy bucket. "Perch hasn't seen anyone else with a cane, and he's been up and down the street a bunch of times. This whole day has been one big wild-goose chase."

Tunie took a deep breath and sighed. Then she hesitated and took another deep breath. And another.

She sniffed at Perch, her eyes widening. "Perch! You smell like hickory smoke—that strong, sweet smell? My old neighbor used to cure meat with hickory woodsmoke, and the fire smelled just like you!"

Peter's head had lifted at Tunie's statement. "That's the smell Horus described! He said the man with the nasal voice smelled like hickory smoke!"

Tunie grinned at Perch. "Do you think you can take us to wherever that hickory smell is coming from?"

Perch flapped happily and took off. Tunie and Peter followed him all the way down the road, toward the end of the commercial stretch. Set back from the street, and near the water's edge, was a wooden building with a sign that read BILLOWING SAILS SHIPPING, INC. From across the small lawn in front of it, Tunie could see purple-gray smoke curling from the building's chimney.

"Excellent work, Perch," Tunie said, scratching him behind his pointed ears. The bat gave her a satisfied look. "Now what? Do we go inside?"

Peter mused. "I think we shouldn't go in, not yet. Once we go in, they might notice us snooping around. Right now they don't even know anybody's looking. Let's wait and see if anyone comes out, so we can follow him."

"Okeydokey." Tunie started washing the window of the corner shop nearest the shipping company. The ruse was starting to seem a little silly, especially now that there was only a half inch of water in the bucket. She didn't know what else to do with herself, though. From this spot across the small green, she could keep an eye on the front door of the shipping company. Peter sat on a bench with his strange headpiece on and WindUp sticking up from the pack beside him, pretending to read his comic book.

"Someone's coming!" Tunie whispered to Peter as the door to the building swung open and a tall, thin man emerged. Peter tilted his head in the man's direction.

"No cane," Tunie said.

The figure turned back and shouted something through the open door.

"It's him!" Peter called softly. "It's got to be! I've never heard such a nasal voice!"

The man stalked out toward the street on long legs. His loose-cut trousers looked worn and slightly dirty, and he wore a scuffed brimmed hat pulled down over narrow eyes. He had a black mustache that curled at the ends. Tunie and Peter struggled to keep up as they followed him down the street.

For a moment, looking over her shoulder for Perch, Tunie thought she saw a face at the second-story window of the shipping company. She squinted. It was only a reflection on the glass.

The mustached man stopped outside a bank as a plump fellow with spectacles and a cane—from his neat suit, obviously a banker—stepped out. The thin man barred the banker's way until the banker reluctantly turned around, and both men went inside.

"Look at the cane!" Tunie said. "This has got to be it. Those two are working together."

Peter nodded. He seemed to be thinking. They watched the bank for a while. The thin man strode out and stepped immediately into a departing streetcar. The children couldn't trail him.

"We could take this information to the police—that the man from the shipping company is one of the kidnappers," Peter said. "It might be enough to earn the reward."

Tunie nodded thoughtfully. "But we don't have any proof, and how would we explain what we know? We can't say a mummy told us to find a man with a nasal voice." Perch glided down and landed expertly on the underside of a shop sign.

Peter agreed. "Yes, I think we need more."

Tunie pushed back her headband, and Peter blinked. "Where did you get that?"

"What?" Tunie asked. She looked around.

"The headband," said Peter, sounding surprised.

"Oh. Perch found it somewhere and brought it to me. He's always bringing me pretty things he finds," Tunie said, smiling fondly at her bat. Perch preened.

"It looks like the one that Dorothy was wearing when she was kidnapped. I mean, from the description of it," Peter said. " 'Light blue ribbon headband.' "

Tunie took the headband off and examined it.

"I never heard anything about what Dorothy was wearing!" she said.

Peter opened his backpack and pulled out a newspaper article. It showed a picture of Dorothy James's parents at the fairgrounds. Dorothy's mother was shading her eyes with a white-gloved hand. Her father was clutching a handkerchief in his fist and speaking to police with an anxious expression on his face. Peter pointed to the description of Dorothy in the article beneath the photograph.

Tunie read it aloud. " 'Last seen wearing a light blue satin party dress and matching blue ribbon headband.' You mean . . . this headband might be Dorothy's?" Her voice grew quieter. "It feels like I've been wearing it for a while. I hate to think about how long she's been missing, and how scared she must be."

"Her family, too," Peter added.

Tunie looked up from the headband. "Perch, where did you get this?"

Perch shrilled and flapped. Tunie nodded.

"He's going to show me tonight," she said.

"Can I come?" Peter asked.

"Sure," said Tunie. "Let's meet in the museum at nine o'clock."

CHAPTER 11

Tunie had a stop to make before she went home that evening. The museum had closed at six, but Tunie let herself in, calling a hello to George before heading down to the mummy exhibit. She couldn't wait to show Horus what she'd brought.

A brownish teardrop leaked from one of Horus's gleaming golden eyes and traveled in a zigzag along the bandages of his face. His hands were clasped before his chest, and his voice trembled with emotion. "These are the most beautiful things I have seen in my endless life."

Tunie surveyed with pride the stack of worn library books she'd found for Horus, a hardbound rainbow tower of reading.

"It's a little of everything," she said. "Pirates, explorers, fairy tales, mysteries, survival, outer space." She didn't want to raise his hopes, so she left out the part about borrowing some books on curses for herself, to see if she and Peter could help Horus. "You can tell me what kinds of stuff you like, and I'll look for more next time. I brought you this pen so you could make me a list. Oh, rats," she said, peering inside the now empty knapsack she'd brought. "I forgot paper."

Tunie was almost knocked off her feet by the little mummy's hug. It was a bit like embracing a papier-mâché mannequin, but it warmed Tunie's heart.

She smiled as Horus stood back and wiped away his tears. He spoke quietly.

"Thank you. I don't deserve your kindness."

"Everybody deserves kindness," Tunie said. She told Horus how she'd noticed earlier that kindness seemed to travel along between people. The butcher whose window she'd cleaned today had given her more chicken than the work was worth, and a woman buying meat had overheard Tunie say she'd use the chicken to make soup for her sick dad. Seeing the butcher's kindness, the woman had given Tunie some bruised tomatoes and somewhat withered vegetables from her stand to make the soup. Tunie was going home to make soup, and there was enough to feed her father and herself for days, so she'd bring some over to old Mrs. Shrubinski and George.

Horus seemed struck by Tunie's observations.

"Kindness travels, indeed," he muttered, resting one

wrapped hand on the book stack. "I'm beginning to realize how incredibly lucky I am to have encountered someone like you, after so many millennia. In fact, I'm beginning to wonder whether it was luck at all."

Tunie slung her bag over her shoulder.

"Maybe it's fate," she said, smiling. Her eyes dropped to the sling stone in Horus's hand. "That's the rock you were holding before. It's for a sling weapon, right? How exactly did you get it out of the display case? Why do you carry it around?"

Horus unfolded his bound fingers, revealing the stone in his palm. "Every night, I use a skillet from that kitchen to smash the display case glass and retrieve this stone. Every day, it disappears from my hand and returns to the case, which mends in a blink, as if it were never shattered."

Then Horus traced the symbol carved into the stone. "This is my only remaining possession. It was a gift from my brother."

Tunie studied the stone and smiled. "Really? And it survived all these centuries? What luck!"

Horus continued, "It reminds me of how badly I treated my brother, and of certain . . . misdeeds."

Tunie stopped smiling. "Oh. Not good luck, then."

Horus closed his fingers over the rock and shook his head. "Well, that's ancient history, so to speak! Can I offer you some tea?"

"Hate to rush, but I need to check on my dad. I'm

meeting Peter back here in a few hours, though. See you soon, Horus!"

"Goodbye, and thank you!" Horus said.

On her way out, Tunie looked back and saw Horus clutching a library book to his skeletal chest. Who cared if he'd been a thief? She was starting to like that little mummy.

CHAPTER 12

"Do not slurp your soup, Randall," Stepma said. Larry, who was sitting at the dining table next to Randall—and had been the one making all the impolite noise—smirked.

Peter had just finished hiding two dinner rolls stuffed with ham in the napkin on his lap. He was feeling grouchy, as Miss Cook had chastised him for getting blood on his shirt and made him change before dinner. As if he'd intentionally set out to injure himself and destroy his own clothing!

His stepmother continued, "I've decided to accompany your father to New York when he leaves, to see him settled. Miss Cook has kindly agreed to look after you all for a few days. Luce will come with us, of course."

"Can I come, too?" Peter asked quickly, looking from his father to his stepmother. If he and Tunie failed, he wouldn't be going to Camp Contraption, and if he wasn't at camp when his father and stepmother left, he'd be stuck home alone with the beastly twins.

"Aw. Is the wittle baby scared to be left alone with us?" Larry taunted.

"Larry," his mother said with disapproval.

Peter gritted his teeth, feeling a flash of fury. "I'd rather be locked in a cage with a grub-eating gorilla than in this house alone with you two. Compared with you, a hairy gorilla is positively *civilized*."

"Peter!" Stepma and his father said at the same time.

"You're the gorilla!" Larry shouted back, spitting a little, his narrow face turning red.

Peter's anger got the best of him. He leaned over his soup toward Larry. "Compared with you, a gorilla is a towering intellectual! Compared with you, a gorilla is a model of hygiene!"

Larry lunged across the table and launched his bowl of soup so it splattered in Peter's face.

Peter wiped his eyes with his sleeve and yelled, "At least a gorilla knows not to waste his food and only throws poo! Oh, wait, I forgot—you do that, too, you poo-flinging primate!"

Peter's father stood and said at full volume, "That's enough! All of you, to your rooms—now!"

Peter managed to keep the ham sandwiches hidden

beneath his shirt as he folded his arms and stormed away. He heard his stepmother usher the twins into their rooms across the hall. In his bedroom, he took the sandwiches, wrapped in his cloth dinner napkin, and placed them in a wooden box so he didn't crush them. He wished he had something more to bring—a thermos of hot chocolate, maybe. The metal thermos they'd had for years was up in a high kitchen cabinet, however; there would be no way to sneak it out.

The thought of the thermos made Peter pause. He had a distant memory of his mother unscrewing the gleaming metal top and pouring chocolate milk into it. She sat on a picnic blanket beside his father, and there was a river nearby. She sang a song about rainbows. Peter thought he remembered chasing a duck and falling in the water. He must have been young. His throat began to tighten, and he pushed the memory away.

He began packing a canvas bag with things he'd need for his meeting with Tunie, when a knock sounded on his door. Peter rapidly shoved the bag under his bed and sat at his desk with WindUp.

"Come in!" Peter called.

Peter's dad walked in and sat on the bed, across from Peter. He took off his glasses and cleaned them on his shirt and put them back on, then took a deep breath. "That was quite a scene you made. Your stepmother is very upset."

Peter shrugged. To his dismay, he could feel the onset

of tears again. He gripped WindUp tightly and said nothing.

His father softly touched one of Peter's clenched hands.

"Listen," he said, "I know it's hard for you, having Stepma in the house. I know you miss your mom. There have been lots of changes here, and it will take a while to get used to them." He cleared his throat. "I can tell that the twins are giving you a hard time."

"I hate them! They're monsters!" Peter hadn't planned on saying that, the words just burst out. "Living with them is worse than living in our old house without Mom!"

Peter's father shook his head. "They lost their dad just like we lost your mother. They've had a rough time, too. People handle things in . . . different ways. Try to be nice to them. For me. Please."

Peter didn't want to argue with his father, so he only nodded. They'd been living with the twins for almost a year, and he hadn't really considered that the twins might be missing their dad. They never mentioned him. Peter's dad almost never mentioned his mother anymore, either. He wouldn't play the music she'd loved on the record player. Sometimes that made it even harder, like she'd never been there in the first place. For a moment, Peter considered asking his dad about the picnic, and whether he'd fallen in the stream. Before he could summon the courage, his father stood and ruffled Peter's hair.

"All right. As punishment, you all will spend the rest of tonight in your rooms, and all day tomorrow helping Miss Cook clean the house."

Peter drooped. He should have known better than to yell at the terrible twins in front of his parents. Now he'd be losing a precious day of detective work because of it. His father gave Peter a hug and left the room, closing the door behind him.

"Well, WindUp," Peter said softly. "We'll have to get as much done as possible tonight." Peter felt slightly guilty about disobeying his father, but he had little choice.

He set WindUp on the bed. The robot played two pleasant music box notes of agreement.

CHAPTER 13

The smell of cinnamon buns wafted out of Eleanor's Elegant Sweet Shoppe as Tunie opened the back door. She'd left her sleeping father right after dinner to come here. It was nearly dusk now, and the orange tone of the dying light made the June air seem even warmer. Tunie knew Miss Eleanor had the baker do as much baking as possible in the evenings during summer, to prevent the shop from growing too hot during the day.

Perch flew up and hung under the eave near the door, sniffing appreciatively.

"The alley's not so stinky tonight," Tunie said, smiling up at her bat. "Keep an eye out for that tomcat, okay?"

Perch settled in comfortably, tucking his wings around him.

Tunie stepped inside. The new baker glanced up from the tray of buns she was putting in the oven, saw that it was Tunie, and wordlessly returned to her work. *Not exactly the friendly sort,* Tunie thought. She was about to go up the stairs when Miss Eleanor swept in from the front of the shop with another woman. The woman wore a cook's uniform with a white hat, collar, and apron front, and darker sleeves. She looked uncomfortably warm compared with Miss Eleanor, neat as ever in a short-sleeved, belted dress with a pretty flower print.

Tunie greeted Miss Eleanor as politely as possible.

"Good evening, ma'am. I thought I'd stop by to see if you had any work for me."

Miss Eleanor nodded curtly to Tunie. "Yes, I can use you tonight. Come with us."

Tunie followed the women upstairs. In Miss Eleanor's small office, Tunie washed her hands with the rose-scented soap while they talked. The cook stood by the desk while Miss Eleanor reviewed a list.

"There are too many folks for me to feed on my own," the cook said. She had an accent Tunie couldn't quite pin down. "Mrs. James wants to provide meals for all them's out looking for her daughter. There's a crew of twenty-five people going over every inch o' that fairground. Our cooking staff's knackered from trying to keep up."

Mrs. James? Dorothy James's mother? Tunie dried her hands slowly, listening.

Miss Eleanor made a sympathetic face. "But they've found nothing?"

"Nothing but gum wrappers and ticket stubs," the cook said, shaking her head sadly. "We all miss that plucky little girl. You'd think she'd be spoiled, daughter of the richest man in town and all, but she isn't a bit. She'll come into the kitchen and read her Nancy Drew books to us while we work. Makes the time pass nicely. It's miserable without her." The cook exhaled heavily. "Mrs. James cries in her bedroom every evening. Mr. James is taking it hard, too. He's always leaving the house at strange hours, late at night. Half the time nobody knows where he is. He's got dark circles under his eyes like a boxer. The family's simply desperate."

Tunie swallowed against the threat of tears.

"It's a terrible shame," Miss Eleanor said. She scratched out numbers and tallied them, then gave a receipt to the cook. The cook counted out payment and handed it to Miss Eleanor, who accepted, saying, "If you send someone for these at ten tomorrow morning, they'll be ready."

"All right, then," said the cook. "I'll see myself out."

She left, and Miss Eleanor passed the list to Tunie.

"I'd like you to write out cards for each of these trays. It shouldn't take you long, so don't expect as much pay as last time. Come see me when you're done."

"Yes, ma'am," Tunie said.

After Miss Eleanor left, Tunie began copying out the list on display cards with a new Moore pen: *Egg Salad, Ham and Cheese, Marble Rye Toast.*

She wondered where Mr. James was going at night.

She pictured Mrs. James, weeping and alone in her bedroom. She didn't dare imagine where Dorothy was.

Tunie bent to her task.

She and Peter would find Dorothy, she resolved, if it was the last thing they did.

CHAPTER 14

Peter dropped his knapsack through the museum window first and then climbed in after it. *Someone really ought to fix that busted latch,* he thought. It was like no one but Peter even saw that it was broken.

The shadowy museum hallways were even more unsettling at night. Peter ran as softly as he could, past rooms marked PLEISTOCENE and DINOSAURS and MARINE LIFE, taking the stairs down two at a time, until he reached the Ancient Egypt exhibit.

He pushed open the exhibit doors. The smoky smell of the place reminded him of the frankincense and myrrh the priest sometimes burned in church. The room was dark, but Peter could see a rectangle of light where the kitchen door stood open.

"Hello? Horus? Tunie?" he called quietly. His voice echoed back. Goose bumps rose on his arms as Peter peered through the dimness at the images of animal-headed men on the walls and the crumbling stone faces of the silent sarcophagi. He fumbled for the light switch and nearly screamed when he flipped it.

Horus stood directly before him, his linen mouth stretched in a wide smile.

"Peter!" The little mummy looked delighted. "You came back!"

"Oh, geez," Peter said with a gasp. "You scared me!"

"Apologies, apologies," said Horus, sounding overjoyed and not at all apologetic. He led Peter to the kitchen. "I've been reading the most wonderful book Tunie brought me!"

In the tiny kitchen, Peter placed his knapsack on the table beside an open book and a mug of tea.

"I have some magazines and newspapers for you," Peter said, first taking out WindUp and setting him on a chair. He pulled out several older issues of *Modern Mechanics* as well as the *Harbortown Gazette* and stacked them on the table.

Horus lifted up a magazine with a photograph of a dirigible on the cover.

"What can it be? Is it in the sky?" the mummy said. He stared with wonder at the airship.

Peter laughed. "It's a dirigible. Wait until you see the issue about submarines." He took out the ham sandwiches. "These are for you and Tunie. She seemed kind of hungry earlier."

"She does appear a bit underfed," Horus agreed. "She should eat them both. But what is that on your shirt?"

Peter plucked his collared shirt away from his chest. There was a large, pinkish stain on the front from the soup Larry had launched at him.

"This is the second shirt my stepbrother has ruined today," Peter said. He told Horus about the twins' bullying and the fight over dinner. "My dad says they're grieving, but so are Tunie and I. We don't act like that."

Horus nodded thoughtfully. "You said Larry is the one who starts the bullying, and he gets Randall involved?"

Peter picked up WindUp and toyed with a dial on his back. "Yeah. Larry's the smart one."

"Ah," said Horus. "Or perhaps he *was* the smart one—until you came along." Horus took a sip of tea. "I was quite jealous of my older brother, Taharqa, you know. He was always telling me I was too little to do things, when what I wanted from him was praise. I yearned for him to acknowledge my strengths." Horus paused. "I understood him too late. Larry might feel the same about you."

Peter was thinking this over when Tunie arrived.

"Sorry I'm late," she said breathlessly. Her eyes widened. "Are those ham sandwiches?"

"They're for you," Peter said. "Miss Cook made me my favorite rolls, and there were a lot of them."

"Thanks, Peter!" Tunie grabbed a sandwich and took a big bite. "Mmmmm." She grinned at Horus. "See? Kindness travels."

"And so should we." Peter zipped WindUp into his knapsack. "Time's running short."

"Wait, let me finish these," Tunie said, reaching for the second sandwich, so she held one in each hand. "I've been wondering, Horus, how you got to be a robber in the first place."

"Ah," said Horus. He seemed reluctant to speak initially, but then he said, "I fell in with a village boy everyone called Turtanu, which was a nickname. It meant something like 'general,'" Horus explained. "Turtanu mocked my brother, Taharqa, and I enjoyed that. I was envious, as I've told Peter. I began following Turtanu and his crowd, joining in their petty crimes."

The mummy looked down at his teacup. Peter thought he'd be blushing, if he were capable.

When Horus spoke, he sounded embarrassed. "To begin with, we stole only from sleeping soldiers, after they'd kicked out and looted the Assyrians. This seemed all right, as the soldiers had just taken the treasures from someone else. Then Turtanu suggested stealing from tombs, and though most people back then would have disagreed, I thought that was all right, too—those people were dead, after all."

Peter asked, "Did you get in trouble? What did your families think?"

Horus shook his head. "I believe they found us too difficult to handle. There was a lot going on at that time. My mother was busy trying to take care of my siblings. She told me not to leave, but she couldn't stop me when I snuck out of our village and followed my brother and his soldiers northeast, along the seacoast. Eventually, Turtanu talked us into looting and burning the homes of Assyrians for fun. I knew I shouldn't, but it was hard to resist Turtanu and his crowd. I spent many weeks ruining people's homes with Turtanu. He would crush their most precious belongings in front of them, for the sheer joy of destruction, and I would join in."

"Oh," said Peter.

Horus looked up at him, a tea-colored shine to his eyes.

"I regret it all," Horus said hoarsely. "I wish I'd followed my conscience, instead of Turtanu. I knew in my heart what we were doing was wrong. If just one person had said as much to me, maybe I would have . . ." Horus trailed off.

Tunie had been listening closely. She looked contemplative.

"I'd bet there's not a person on this earth who doesn't regret something they've done," she said with such conviction that Peter wondered what it was Tunie regretted.

The mummy turned to Peter. "There is a chance your stepbrother Randall feels the same way I did, but he's allowing his brother to lead him in his bullying. Talking to both of them might help, Peter."

Peter nodded. "I'll try."

Horus attempted to say something but appeared overwhelmed by emotion. He wiped a tear dripping down his bandages. Then he cleared his throat and glanced at the clock. "I know I'm keeping you. Don't stay out too late. I look forward to seeing you again."

"For sure," said Peter. "We'll be back tomorrow." He shouldered his pack. "Bye, Horus."

Tunie gave the little mummy a hug and headed for the door. She turned back to wave at Horus. "Don't worry. We'll come to talk to you!"

None of them knew that on Tunie's next visit, she wouldn't be talking.

She'd be screaming.

CHAPTER 15

"All the way up there?" Tunie said.

Perch squeaked an affirmative.

Peter tilted his head back.

"Maybe there's another entrance?" he said.

Tunie wiped a drip of sweat off her cheek with the back of her hand. "The building is locked from the inside."

They were eyeing a rickety ladder that ran up the side of an abandoned cinder-block building. Apparently, Perch had found the light blue ribbon headband somewhere on the roof. As luck would have it, this former factory stood a block and a half down from the three-story brick police station. The building was in bad repair. Even by the weak light of the moon, Peter could see the cinder blocks were crumbling, and the ladder rungs were patchy with rust. It didn't look sturdy.

Peter had been feeling uneasy ever since they left the museum. This neighborhood beyond the police station had a neglected appearance. They'd passed a couple of abandoned buildings like this one, shops that had closed down when customers had no money to spend. Through the open doorways of vacant stores, he'd seen homeless folks huddled in the shadows. He knew loads of people were out of work; the poor economy had displaced whole families. Still, it was spooky to hear voices murmuring in the dark. Every now and then, a police car would drive by them, siren wailing. Peter couldn't shake the sense they were being watched, and the idea that Perch was leading them to where he'd found the headband—to the place Dorothy's kidnapper might have dragged her— only made the night creepier.

"I'll go first," Tunie offered, and started climbing up the ladder before Peter could object, testing each rung with her foot before putting her weight on it. He saw her silhouetted form move quickly up the ladder and disappear over the roof ledge. Peter squinted. The evening was so warm and muggy, it seemed the thick atmosphere was dimming the stars.

"Made it!" Tunie called down in a stage whisper.

Peter followed, the rusty metal flaking beneath his damp fingers. He was breathing hard by the time he reached the roof. Tunie gave him a relieved smile when he appeared.

"Phew!" Peter said, wiping his hands on his pants. "I wasn't sure that was going to hold."

Suddenly Perch, who had been looping overhead, let out an urgent squeak. It was followed by a loud crack.

Peter quickly looked down. As he watched, the lower half of the ladder fell away from the wall with a groan of twisting metal. It dangled for a moment and then crashed to the ground.

Was it Peter's imagination, or was there something moving in the shadows below?

Tunie rushed over. "What was that?"

They both looked down at the street. The electric streetlamps illuminated portions of the road, but outside their circles of light, everything was murky. Peter blinked. Whatever it was had vanished.

"The ladder broke."

Tunie looked anxious. "Did you see someone?"

"I'm not sure. Maybe not. I guess we'll have to find another way down," Peter said. He pulled WindUp from his knapsack, slid aside a small door on the robot's stomach, and flipped a switch. The metal was slippery beneath his sweaty fingers. Light shone out from WindUp's middle.

"Swell!" said Tunie, sounding impressed. "Now we can see!"

"I wanted WindUp to be a useful companion," Peter said. "He's helped me out of some jams with the twins, that's for sure."

Peter lifted the robot and used him to scan the rooftop.

It was flat, with cylindrical smokestacks here and there. On the far side there was what looked like a shed with a door and a sign that read EXIT TO STAIRWELL.

Tunie said, "Perch, will you show us where you found the headband? And then let's get over to the station, fast. This place is scary. I'll feel a lot better with some police around."

Perch sailed over to the small roofed structure and landed on a railing that ran along one side of it. He piped. Tunie and Peter followed.

"This is where you found the headband?" Tunie asked when they reached the bat. She looked at the shed's peeling paint, the empty rooftop, and shrugged. "There's nothing here."

Peter studied the railing near Perch's tiny claws.

"Wait, look," he said. "Some of the rust has been scraped away along the top and side of this railing, see?" He pointed.

"Oh my goodness!" Tunie clapped a hand over her mouth, and tears sprang to her blue eyes.

"What?" Peter asked, alarmed.

Tunie pointed. On the wall beneath the railing, scratched into the peeling paint, were the words

HELP ME—D.J.

Tunie's voice was shaking. "D.J. . . . ."

Peter and Tunie exchanged a look and said in unison, "*Dorothy James.*"

CHAPTER 16

This whole adventure was suddenly too real for Tunie's taste.

"This is enough, right? I mean, for us to go to the police and get the reward," Tunie said.

"Definitely," Peter agreed. He sounded as edgy as she felt.

"Okay." Tunie swallowed. "Let's go now. There are always a few officers working the night shift."

Peter stood behind Tunie as she tugged at the locked door. She froze.

"What if Dorothy James is down there, in this building?" Tunie said. "Or what if her kidnapper is? What if both kidnappers are in there?"

Peter let out a breath. "I don't know what else we can do. It's the only way down."

"The door is locked." Tunie rattled the knob uselessly.

Peter looked closely at the lock. "I can pick this kind."

He opened a hatch on WindUp and took out what looked like a small metal stick.

"Really?" Tunie blinked.

"Sure," Peter said, sliding the piece of metal into the lock and moving it around. "It's a skeleton key lock. Not the most secure design."

Tunie had to admit, Peter certainly was handy.

"Got it!" Peter said, sounding pleased. With a click, the door swung open. Hot air, even warmer than the steamy summer evening, wafted out. A staircase descended into darkness. He held out WindUp. They could see only a few steps, to where the stairs turned.

Perch flew in and vanished. Peter and Tunie waited uneasily for the bat's return.

In less than a minute, Perch flapped out from the doorway. He made some high-pitched noises, and Tunie's shoulders relaxed slightly.

"I think it's safe," she said.

She reached for Peter's hand. He tucked WindUp under one arm, with his light shining down. Both of their hands were clammy with sweat. Each of them held on to a railing and stepped down into the blackness. Tunie wished she were almost anywhere else—mopping in the museum or lying on her mattress, listening to her father's horrible cough.

"Geez, I can't see anything but our feet," Peter said. His voice sounded loud in the empty space.

"Me neither," Tunie said, keeping a firm grip on the railing and Peter's hand. The air was dank and smelled of mildew. They made their way slowly, one step at a time. It seemed to take ages.

"Tunie, you lost your mom, too, right?" Peter said in the gloom.

"Yes, a little more than two years ago."

"Do you still miss her?"

"All the time."

"Me too. My dad never talks about her, though. He even put all her records up in the closet. She used to play music all the time. Now it's always quiet." His voice sounded forlorn.

Tunie squeezed his hand. "He hasn't forgotten her, trust me. He doesn't want to upset you."

"I guess."

"If you want to talk about her, talk about her. I bet he'll follow your lead."

Perch squeaked, and finally Tunie's foot found the concrete floor. Peter swept WindUp back and forth, and Tunie waved one hand before her, searching out obstacles. Ahead, a small square of glass glowed dimly.

"There's the door," Tunie whispered. She couldn't explain why she was whispering.

At last, they pushed open the door to the moonlit outdoors, which seemed much brighter after the black interior of the building. A police car came screaming down the street, lights flashing. Tunie and Peter broke into a run.

The front door to the police station was open, and they raced up the front steps. Perch flew up and vanished near the gutter. Only when they were inside did they stop, panting. Tunie was grateful for the brightly lit lobby, and the great, familiar uniformed officer who greeted them with concern.

"Tunie? What's the matter, kids?"

"Officer Hill!" Tunie said with relief. She knew him. He was friendly with her father—they'd fought together in France during the war. The solidly built officer had children of his own—two girls. They'd come to dinner once, back when her mother was alive. Tunie felt she'd never been so glad to see anyone in her life.

Tunie and Peter spoke breathlessly over one another, explaining that they thought they knew who Dorothy James's kidnapper was, and that they had evidence to hand over to the police.

The big policeman nodded.

"Okay, kids, okay," said Officer Hill. "You both seem a little spooked. I'm going to take you to Detective Dedrick Shade. He's here tonight, and he's been working pretty hard to crack that case. You can tell him about it, and I'll get you something to drink. Then we'll give your parents a ring, all right?"

With gentle hands, he guided them down the hallway.

Tunie was glad to be safe inside, but still feeling fretful. Her father wasn't reachable, and she didn't want the police to worry him by showing up at their door. Also, she never liked leaving Perch out alone. Of course he could handle himself, but he was prey to all kinds of things, including cats and owls.

As if he could sense her anxiety, Peter gave her hand a squeeze.

"It's going to be all right now," he said.

"I hope they find Dorothy," Tunie said softly.

Officer Hill patted her on the back. "I'm sure Detective Shade will find her. Just think—if you're right about what you know, Mr. James will give you that reward money, too."

Officer Hill led them to an airless paneled office with two hard chairs in front of a desk. A filing cabinet stood in a corner with a great, overgrown tangle of a plant on top of it. Behind the unadorned desk, facing the chairs, sat a bald man with a lean jaw. His close-set eyes and sharp nose and chin made it seem like all his features were being pulled toward a point just beyond his face. The brass nameplate on the desk indicated that he was Detective Dedrick Shade.

"Detective Shade, this is Tunie Webster, and this here is Peter . . . what's your surname, son?"

"Bartholomew," Peter said. Tunie realized they hadn't known each other's last names. It seemed odd; they'd shared a lot in the short time they'd spent together.

Officer Hill repeated, "Peter Bartholomew. They have some information for you on your Dorothy James case. Sounds like you might crack it tonight."

Detective Shade looked them over curiously with his pale blue eyes, which were so near to each other they almost crossed. "You two are out awfully late. This must be important. Please, sit down. I'm interested in your story."

Officer Hill encouraged Tunie and Peter to sit. Then he asked Peter for his parents' phone number. Tunie had to admit that she and her father had no phone. Detective Shade listened intently.

"I'll call Peter's parents and bring you all some lemonade," Officer Hill said, and closed the door behind him.

Detective Shade leaned toward them.

In a noncommittal tone, he said, "Well, then. Let's hear it."

Tunie took a breath. "We met someone at the museum who overheard Dorothy being kidnapped but didn't see it," she began.

Detective Shade drummed his fingers. "And who is this person? Why isn't he or she here?"

Peter said, "Um, he's afraid to come forward. But it doesn't matter. We found this."

He reached over and pulled the light blue ribbon headband off of Tunie's head. He was handing it across the desk to Detective Shade when Officer Hill opened the door. A look of irritation flashed across Detective Shade's face.

Spying the headband, Officer Hill whistled. His shaggy gray eyebrows lifted.

"That's the headband, Dedrick! Oh-ho, you've got him now!" Officer Hill said. Then he turned to the kids with a smile. "I'm afraid we're out of lemonade. How about iced tea?"

The kids accepted, and Officer Hill left again.

Tunie and Peter told Detective Shade where Perch found the headband. They described at length the wall with the initials and the words *Help me* scratched into the paint, and told the detective about the nasal-voiced man who had come out of the Billowing Sails Shipping building.

Detective Shade's brows lowered, as if he was contemplating a problem.

"You don't have a name for this man, or anything to go on except that your anonymous witness—which will never fly in court, by the way—said it was 'someone with a nasal voice.' That could be anyone with a cold, really," Detective Shade said, rubbing one hand along the top of his bare head.

"But that clue about the rooftop—and the message in the paint—that's quite good information. The headband, too," he said, taking the light blue ribbon headband off his desk and placing it carefully in a drawer. "I'm going to look into this personally. Now, I need to ask you for a favor," he said. "I want you to keep this information to yourself. Tell no one—not even your own parents."

Peter frowned. His face was still bright pink from their sprint to the station, and Tunie could see the hair above his ears was damp with perspiration. "Why can't we tell our parents? Won't they wonder why the police are calling them in the middle of the night? We can tell them not to talk about it."

Detective Shade was shaking his head forcefully. "Even one more person knowing is one person too many. Right now, the element of surprise is on my side, but if anyone finds out—why, the evidence could be destroyed! I need to sneak up on this man, see if he'll lead me to the people he's working with. Young Dorothy's life may hang in the balance. I'm counting on you to preserve her safety. You must maintain complete silence. You can tell your parents you were here because . . . you were helping an elderly person who had been robbed. Will you do that for me?"

Peter had fallen quiet during Shade's explanation and didn't respond. Tunie answered for both of them.

"Yes, we won't tell anyone what we've found. But . . . you will let Mr. James know? That we helped solve the case? Because—"

Detective Shade nodded vigorously. "The reward money, of course. You have my word, it will be yours if this information leads to something—and I'm sure Officer Hill will back me up on that. All right?"

There was a knock on the door, and Officer Hill himself appeared, this time with two cups of iced tea and a man with tousled gray hair who looked like an older version of Peter, but with glasses.

Officer Hill said, "Detective Shade, this is Professor Bartholomew, Peter's father. I've taken down his contact information."

"Dad!" Peter cried. He ran to his father and they embraced. "I can't believe how fast you got here! Can we go home?"

"Sure, son," Peter's dad said. He looked over at Tunie. Tunie thought he must have sensed the sudden wave of despair she felt at the prospect of being left alone here.

"Can we give you a ride home, dear?" he said to Tunie.

"Oh, yes, thanks! I live right near here. It'll only take a minute."

"Actually, I'd like to talk with the girl some more," Detective Shade said impatiently, but Tunie was already on her feet. She turned to Officer Hill.

"Officer Hill, thanks for the tea," Tunie said. She accepted the cup and took a large swallow. It was terrible, but she was so thirsty she drank it down. "I'm sorry to rush off. I'll come back tomorrow, but I need to get back to my dad. He's going to be very worried."

And even though it was a short walk through the woods, she didn't want to go home by herself in the dark, not tonight.

Officer Hill nodded. "Of course, my dear. I'd be worried sick if my girls were out this late."

Officer Hill led them to the lobby. Detective Shade stood and went with them. Tunie noticed he walked with a strange, limping gait, though he attempted to hide it. She tried not to stare, but Tunie observed that one of his shoes seemed to fit strangely, sticking out at an awkward angle from his ankle.

Suddenly Peter said, "My knapsack! I left it in Detective Shade's office!" He darted down the hall, calling, "I'll be right back!"

It took Peter a surprisingly long time to return. Tunie started to wonder what on earth he was doing, and the adults were beginning to look around with concern. He finally reappeared, breathless and apologizing, saying he'd gotten turned around. Peter, Tunie, and Professor Bartholomew stepped out into the sultry night. Peter's dad led them to a car parked in front of the station.

"Hop in, kids," he said, and Tunie followed Peter inside. In a single smooth motion, Perch dove down from the sky and right into the open bag at Tunie's belt. Tunie was relieved to see her pocket-sized friend, and she gave him a pat on his furry head before climbing into the car. It was the first time she'd ever ridden in an automobile. Through its glass window, Tunie caught sight of Detective Shade, leaning out of the station doorway, watching them.

She didn't see him return to his office. She didn't see him remove his shoe. She didn't hear him pace around his office on his peg leg. *Tap, tap, tap.*

CHAPTER 17

Peter noticed how Tunie gripped the leather edge of her seat as the car bounced along the dirt road toward her house, headlights exposing the dusty trunks of trees.

"You're the only people I know who have a car," Tunie said, her voice rising at a particularly sharp jounce. "Fancy."

Peter and his father laughed.

Peter's dad said, "It isn't ours. I borrowed it from the university president, who came by for coffee tonight."

"Oh," Tunie said. "That's my house, straight ahead." She turned to Peter. "Can we talk tomorrow?"

Peter started to say yes, but his father interrupted. "Sorry, Tunie, but Peter's grounded tomorrow. He'll be cleaning all day as punishment for fighting with his stepbrothers, and he'll probably be grounded all next week for the stunt he pulled tonight, sneaking out like this. That old fellow was lucky you were there to see the person rob him, though."

Tunie was silent for a moment as the car pulled to a stop, the headlight beams revealing what was little more than a hovel. *This was where Tunie lived?* Peter was stunned. His own cramped townhouse seemed like a palace by comparison. He felt ashamed all over again for how greedy he'd been at first about the reward money. Tunie's mom was gone, and she was worried she might lose her dad, too. Peter couldn't let her become an orphan. He'd give her a bigger share of the reward, he decided. He'd take just enough to go to camp. After all, without Tunie and Perch, he'd be nowhere with his investigation.

Tunie didn't exit right away. Instead, she scooted forward on her seat.

"Professor Bartholomew," she said in an urgent voice, "I've seen Peter's stepbrothers gang up on him. Two to one. They're mean and they beat him and . . . well, a person can't blame him for fighting. I only wish I could be there every time, to make it fair. And also"—she spoke in a rush, to keep Peter's dad from interrupting—"the only reason Peter was out tonight was because of me. My dad's really sick, and Peter was helping me . . . finish some of my dad's work. I asked Peter for his help. I really hope you won't blame him for lending me a hand. Peter's a . . . well, he's a decent, good, and kind person. I'm the only one who should be in trouble," she said. With that, she opened the door and slid out.

"Thanks again for the ride," she said, and slammed the door shut, hurrying into the tiny house.

"Bye, Tunie!" Peter called through the window.

Peter's dad was silent for a moment. Then he turned in his seat, looking over his shoulder as he backed up the car.

"Well, Peter," he said finally, "it sure seems like you've found a friend."

Peter thought of how Tunie had stood up to the twins when they were attacking him, and how she'd defended him just now. She was the kind of friend he'd wished for all year.

"Yeah," Peter agreed. "Tunie's pretty great."

He spent the rest of the ride home answering his father's questions as best he could without mentioning Dorothy James or her kidnapping, while still mulling over how he'd sneak out the next day. He felt a jolt of excitement every time he thought of how, among the monstrous vines of the plant in Detective Shade's office, he'd hidden an intercom device he'd made. WindUp could receive radio waves from it. It had a Swedish nickel-cadmium battery in it that wouldn't last too long, though. Peter needed to get over to the Harbortown Police Station as soon as possible and try to get near enough with the receiver to listen in on Shade before the battery ran out. There was something about the detective that Peter simply didn't like.

CHAPTER 18

With a satisfied sigh, Horus closed the book he'd been reading in the museum's tiny kitchen. The novel was a mystery about someone named Hercule Poirot, and Horus had been transported by the story to the point that he'd entirely forgotten where he was. What a blessing!

Something unusual was happening to the mummy. He felt a kind of unfolding in his chest, a softness, something gentle. He'd wanted to do something for Tunie, but what? His mother had liked sweets, dates, and honey. Horus had a sweet tooth himself. Yet he had no way to procure such things for Tunie. He'd grown to be a fair artist, doodling away the decades. Perhaps he could draw something for her. As long as he created something from things left behind and not from the exhibit, it wouldn't disappear.

He decided he'd ask her what kinds of things she liked, on her next visit.

Through the open doorway, the exhibit was silent and empty, the other sarcophagi on display showing impassive carved faces from dynasties earlier than his own. There was a mummy from a Middle Kingdom necropolis, another from the Second Intermediate Period. None of them still lingered in this world. Horus placed his wrapped hand on the book's worn cover. It was worth more to him than all the treasures he'd stolen while he was alive, more than gold, more than jewelry. The moment he'd realized Tunie and Peter could see him, he'd felt the buzz of opportunity like he hadn't since his pillaging days. He still could hardly believe that Tunie had brought the books. He'd already given her the information she wanted; he hadn't been certain she'd return, but she'd kept her word. He wished he'd known her while he was alive, instead of Turtanu. Someone like Tunie could bring out the good in a person, he thought. Maybe he would have been a better boy.

Maybe.

Horus looked down at the smooth sling stone in his hand. He remembered the last time he'd used the rock. He could almost smell the smoke from the flaming houses, hear the shouts of his brother's bare-chested soldiers. While he and Horus were looting, Turtanu had spied a young boy with a bow and decided he wanted it. The boy began to run when Turtanu shouted at him. Turtanu grabbed Horus's sling from his hand.

"Give me the rock," Turtanu demanded. "I'll stop him."

Horus hesitated. The rock was heavy and dangerous. Turtanu could kill the boy if he hit him in the head.

"I said give it to me!" Turtanu shouted. He snatched the stone from Horus's hand and swung it in the sling. Horus didn't stop him. Horus watched the rock fly through the air, a dark thing arcing against the blue sky, then heard a cry of pain and saw the boy collapse in the distance. Turtanu shouted with triumph and ran to catch him. Horus held his breath, terrified that the boy might be dead, and was greatly relieved to see him stagger to his feet.

Horus gazed down sorrowfully at the carved stone in his wrapped hand, much worn now. No point in dwelling, in wishing for things to be different. He wasn't a good boy then, and he wasn't any kind of boy now. Horus pondered, the hopeful feeling Tunie had roused in him beginning to fade. He supposed he should try to get what he could from Tunie and Peter before they grew tired of Horus, bored with outings to the museum. Before they realized they could never help that poor kidnapped girl, that two children and a clever bat could never hold their own against evil like those men. Horus knew from experience. After all, he'd been evil himself.

CHAPTER 19

When Tunie crept in the door, her house was dark and silent. The air smelled of leftover soup. She could hear her father's labored breathing coming from his room. Tunie locked the door and pushed a stool beneath the doorknob, knowing that neither of these devices would keep out a persistent intruder. The idea of Dorothy's kidnapper roaming free out there was starting to make her feel a little on edge.

Perch, however, seemed entirely untroubled. He flew directly to his nook and fell asleep, issuing tiny bat snores.

Tunie realized they'd forgotten to tell Detective Shade that Horus had heard a tapping sound during Dorothy James's kidnapping, and that the banker with the cane was a possible conspirator. Tunie wished she could talk to Peter about everything; their promise to Detective Shade had prevented them from discussing the case on the way home. She decided she'd return to the police station tomorrow and make sure the police had all the details.

To take her mind off kidnappers, Tunie read a thin textbook on curses, trying to find something that might help Horus. Unfortunately, the book was about how to place curses on people, and sounded dodgy even to Tunie—tying string around a rotten cabbage and spinning it over a candle? Eventually exhaustion took over, and Tunie fell asleep fully dressed. She slept fitfully for a few hours and woke in the early gray dawn. She sat straight up and looked at the door. The stool was still in place, and her father was snoring in the next room. It was too early yet to head back to the station.

Tunie stretched and cleaned herself up as quietly as she could. Then she sat near the window on the other stool, flipping through a different illustrated book of curses: seasonal curses, curses of enemies, curses of familiars. Tunie didn't like to think about that one. As if reading her mind, Perch flapped over, hung upside down on a nearby towel bar for company, and snoozed.

Tunie turned to a page with a full-color illustration of a mummy beneath a full moon. The words *Everlasting Regret* were beneath the moon. *Wait a minute,* Tunie thought. *That sounds like Horus's curse!* She read on, her heart beating faster.

"The Eternity of Regret, or Everlasting Regret, is a curse one may place upon the selfish and unworthy at a moment when the cursed one is performing an evil deed. Although it is meant to last forever, it is said that acts of selflessness and kindness, performed under the eye of a full moon, may, over time, alleviate the curse."

Tunie peered out the window. It was a foggy morning, and the sun was a white glow barely visible between the trees. If she went soon enough, she could visit Horus and tell him about the curse before the museum opened.

First, though, she'd pick some wild strawberries for breakfast. Her father needed something to eat besides day-olds. She'd seen some strawberries in the grassy patch behind their house a few days ago; they should be ripe by now. This was something else to be thankful for, Tunie thought. The founder of the museum had wanted to preserve the property's natural environment. Though their house was cramped, Tunie felt lucky to live surrounded by greenery. Fresh fruit would do her dad some good.

Perch woke up, blinked a few times, and squeaked to be let outside.

"Would you mind checking to see if anyone's around?" Tunie asked Perch. "I know it sounds crazy, but I'm afraid the kidnapper might be lurking out there."

Perch squeaked his assent, and Tunie cracked the door open for him. After about five minutes, he returned.

"All clear?" Tunie asked him. Perch nodded his furry little head.

"Great!" Tunie said with relief. She quietly left the house and walked around back to the damp, grassy clearing. The strawberries were red and ripe. It took Tunie only a half hour to pick the berries, rinse them, and leave them in a bright bowl with a note for her father. Yet that delay made all the difference.

CHAPTER 20

Peter went downstairs early the next morning, before anyone but Miss Cook was awake. He gulped down toast and then asked her for his chores. This punishment was harsher than his father intended; Peter had more pressing things to do that day than anyone knew.

"If you have any one-person jobs that would keep me away from the twins for a while, I'd appreciate it," Peter said gloomily.

Miss Cook looked sympathetic.

She handed him a notebook and a pen. "I need an inventory of what's in the storeroom downstairs. You can lock the door to the cellar while you're in there, if you like."

He grinned. It was too good to be true! He'd be on his

own and out of sight—perfect for sneaking away. Peter thanked Miss Cook enthusiastically and went down to the basement with his knapsack and the notebook. He set WindUp to play a happy tune, for company, and began a detailed inventory list of all the dry and canned goods lining the shelves: Campbell's soup, Heinz vegetable salad, baking powder. He worked as neatly and quickly as possible; if luck was on his side, he'd be able to do his chores here and also slip out to the police station without anyone knowing.

Peter's father soon knocked on the cellar door. Peter climbed up and unlocked it. His father stood at the top of the stairwell and looked down at Peter through his glasses.

"Miss Cook tells me she gave you an inventory task that should keep you busy for a few hours," his father said.

"Yes, sir. It'll be a while before I finish," Peter said agreeably.

His father eyed Peter warily, seeming somehow mistrustful of Peter's calm acceptance.

"You know you can't just sit down there and work on WindUp. Your stepmother and I are going to run errands now, but I'll check on you when we come back this afternoon."

Peter tried to look as innocent as possible.

"I promise I'll get it done, sir," he said.

His father nodded and left.

Peter waited, counting cans until he heard his parents leave through the front door. He tucked WindUp inside his knapsack. Then he pulled a storage box over to the small garden-level window near the top of the wall, climbed up on it, and squeezed out. The window exited to a narrow alley between Peter's building and the next. A woman walking her dog on the nearby sidewalk looked at him strangely as he emerged from the base of their building. Peter smiled and jogged down the alley to the street behind his house, hoping to avoid his parents. He didn't have money for a streetcar, and the police station was about two miles away. There was no time to lose.

The morning was already hot, the air close. The boulevard that ran by the museum and the police station was busier than it had been the night before. Peter had to wait a long time to cross the streets on the way to the station. He kept glancing around, worried his father and stepmother might pass by and discover where Peter was before he had a chance to eavesdrop on Detective Shade.

Peter made it to the brick police station without incident, however. He glanced around and then dove behind the shrubbery below the window he thought belonged to Shade's office. It was cooler out of the sun, but not much. Peter was sweating as he drew WindUp from his pack and fiddled with some dials. There was a crackling sound and some static. Peter waited. Was it working but the office was empty? Or had something gone wrong with his design? He hoped it was only that Detective Shade hadn't come in yet.

Peter pushed a sharp branch away from his face and settled in the dirt, with his back against the building, the bush screening him from view. He opened a box of animal crackers to eat while he waited.

"Well, WindUp," Peter said, "we're getting pretty good at spying on people. If I can't become an inventor, maybe I'll be a detective instead. I'd deal with all kinds of crooks—hatchet men, grifters, bank robbers, even murderers!"

He gestured enthusiastically with his cracker at this last word and bumped WindUp, who emitted a faint chime. Peter was on the verge of meeting true criminals, even earlier than he expected.

CHAPTER 21

In a cupboard beneath the sink in the undersized museum kitchen, Horus had discovered a treasure. It was a paint-spattered plank of plywood with a splintery side and pockmarks along the bottom. Someone had stashed it in the cupboard's shadowy recesses, and Horus noticed it when he was hiding his beloved library books.

"However did I miss this?" Horus said aloud, setting aside his carved sling stone and dragging the plank out onto the floor with delight. He'd rifled through everything in the exhibit and the kitchen more than once, out of sheer boredom, and had never seen this before. Someone must have left it within the last month; he hadn't thoroughly searched for a few weeks.

Horus clapped. "It's perfect!"

He'd been wishing for a canvas of some kind, in order to make a surprise gift for Tunie. He had no way to go in search of a present, but he did have some artistic skill. It wasn't much, but it was all he had to offer.

Horus thought back to the gift his older brother had given him. Horus must have been about seven, and Taharqa gave him the braided sling he'd fashioned himself and the rock to throw, for practice. The rock was a smooth river stone, and his brother had carved a unique symbol into it. His brother set the rock and sling in Horus's small hand.

"You place a rock here, and you use this sling to throw it very far, like this." His brother demonstrated. He placed the rock in the sling and whirled it. It whistled through the air, gray against the blue sky, and landed in the distant dirt with a brown puff. Horus ran to retrieve it.

When he returned, grinning, Horus looked into Taharqa's big brown eyes, so like his own.

"Now I can go fight with you!" Horus said.

Taharqa laughed. "Ah, you're still a child," he said, almost wistfully. "This is for play."

"I'm not a baby! I can fight, too!" Horus placed the stone in the sling and tried to throw it, but it hit the ground not far from them and bounced aside.

"It takes a lot of practice. You have time." Taharqa sounded melancholy. He stood up, ruffling Horus's hair before he left.

"You should remain a child as long as you can," he said.

Horus had glowered with resentment. He'd thought his brother was mocking him. Later he realized what war involved: violence, bloodshed, vengefulness, and rage. On plaques in his exhibit, he'd read about men who had spent their entire lives fighting. He knew now his older brother hadn't wanted Horus to hurry into that life. Such misunderstandings were what had led Horus to follow Turtanu around.

Horus placed one linen-wrapped hand flat on the plywood, brushing off dust and paint flakes. He would sketch out what he wanted to paint with the pen Tunie had brought him, and figure it out from there.

The mummy sat in front of the blank piece of wood, thinking. What should he paint? It had to be meaningful. It was nearly morning, and as he thought it over, he felt the strange pull of his curse calling him back toward his sarcophagus. He knew if he didn't obey, the curse would eventually yank him there and whisk the plywood back into the cupboard and out of sight.

He slid the plywood back in its place himself and padded over to his sarcophagus, holding the pen. If someone were to see it, he or she wouldn't question its presence. One would assume a visitor had dropped it. The magic of the curse worked to keep Horus's presence hidden from everyone but Tunie and Peter. He wanted to hold the pen and take time to mull over what he would paint.

This was something else Tunie had done for him; she'd provided happy things to occupy his mind during the slow daylight hours. If only he could do something as nice for her.

This was what Horus was thinking when he realized someone was prowling around the exhibit.

CHAPTER 22

Perch scouted the woods and path to the museum, then let Tunie know it was safe. She was exhausted, and her eyes felt dry from too little sleep. Even Perch flapped droopily alongside her. Still, Tunie felt encouraged. Things were looking up! There might be a way for Horus to alleviate his curse. She and Peter had reported what they knew about Dorothy James's kidnapping, and everything was in good hands. She hoped the police would find Dorothy quickly. With the reward money, Tunie could finally take her father to see a doctor—a good one—and pay for whatever treatment he needed. There would probably be money left over, too, enough for real food. She imagined a fish-and-chips dinner, and a fresh spinach salad, and ice cream for dessert! She wiped her forehead on her shirtsleeve as she opened the door to the museum. Ice cream sounded dreamy. It was a hot, sticky day already, a harbinger of the overwarm summer to come.

The door creaked open, and Tunie called up to George. "It's me—Tunie! I just forgot something down here last night."

"All righty, Tunie," George yelled down the stairwell.

Perch gave a yawn, showing the little white needles of his teeth. There was a dark nook in the stairwell, with a bar and hangers for coats, that made a nice snoozing spot for Perch.

"You need a nap," Tunie said, giving Perch a gentle pat on the head. "Why don't you sleep a little? I'll see if Horus is still, uh, awake or animated or whatever."

Horus had said something about being able to move only at night. It was still quite early in the morning— six o'clock—and the museum wouldn't open for another three hours. Given the inscrutable magic of his curse, she wasn't sure if he'd be up and about or lying unmoving in his sarcophagus. Tunie opened the door to the Ancient Egypt exhibit and closed it behind her, flipping on the light switch.

"Horus?" Tunie called softly. The exhibit was still. Then Tunie thought she heard a sound coming from the employee kitchen.

"Oh, good!" Tunie said. She hurried to the kitchen. She couldn't wait to tell Horus that there might be a way out of his eternal punishment. There would be a full moon that very night. If he could perform some act of kindness, it might help free him from his curse!

Stepping through the doorway, Tunie gasped. It wasn't Horus in the kitchen. She recognized the tall figure in his brimmed hat and unclean trousers. The thin, mustached man grinned evilly, grabbing Tunie and smothering her face with a cloth that smelled like some kind of awful chemical. Tunie drew in a breath and screamed for Perch, but the cloth muffled the sound, and the deep breath only made her inhale more of the chemical.

The world went dark.

CHAPTER 23

As Horus lay in his sarcophagus, tears ran from his eyes. He heard Tunie's muffled scream and that unpleasantly familiar nasal voice. The thin man had peered into Horus's sarcophagus when he arrived, presumably looking for Tunie, before hiding in the kitchen. Horus had tried to call out to warn Tunie, but the rising sun had rendered him mostly immobile. If only Tunie had come a few minutes earlier, when Horus could have stood by her and masked her presence with his curse!

Horus could still move his limbs a little within his sarcophagus. He managed to tear a blank page from the back of a library book beneath him, and uncovered the pen he'd hidden, too. Horus sketched a perfect likeness of the thin, mustached man. His hand was stiffening even as he drew. Horus managed to write:

THIS MAN KIDNAPPED DOROTHY JAMES AND TUNIE WEBSTER

But every second, the lettering became more difficult, until finally his hands froze and the paper and pen fell down into the shadowy sarcophagus, where his message would never be seen. Horus was trapped, unable to move until the sun set. He could not stand the thought of sweet Tunie in the clutches of that wicked man. Horus's papery chest filled with despair, and the last tear he was able to cry slid down his bandages and dripped away.

This was easily the worst day of his unnaturally long life.

CHAPTER 24

Peter had been sitting in the shrubbery for more than an hour, dripping sweat tickling his lower back. To pass the time, he daydreamed about living with his mother—alive and healthy!—and father in the Blue Ridge Mountains. Peter knew in real life his mother would never come back. He was stuck with the twins for the rest of his life. This was his daydream, he thought stubbornly. He could envision what he wanted.

Suddenly there was a loud crackling from WindUp, and Peter lowered the volume, turning the dial and holding his ear to the speaker on WindUp's back. Finally!

"Thanks, Doris," came Detective Shade's voice. "Oh, and, Doris—I'm expecting a visit this morning from a gentleman named Mr. Curtis Reid. You can show him in when he arrives."

The woman, Doris, murmured a reply.

For a long while, Peter waited impatiently. He heard paper rustling, Detective Shade blowing his nose, and drawers banging. At last, a door creaked and Peter heard a recognizably nasal voice.

"Heya, Peg Leg," the nasal voice said in greeting. Peter flattened his back as hard as he could against the wall, to keep out of sight. He knew that voice! It was the thin, mustached man—the one they'd followed from the shipping company!

"Reid. Close the door behind you," Detective Shade said tersely.

Did this mean Peter and Tunie were right, and Curtis Reid was Dorothy James's kidnapper? There were the sounds of the door closing and of a chair being dragged across the floor.

Peter waited for Detective Shade to accuse Reid, to handcuff and arrest him. To his surprise, the men began to speak in low whispers instead. Peter turned up the volume on WindUp as loud as he dared, and listened. He heard a slurping sound and then a cough.

"This is the worst coffee I've ever tasted," Reid said loudly. "I should have asked for dog soup!" Then, more quietly, "I've got the girl. Nabbed her this morning in the museum, just as you suggested. Cleaning up after her useless dad," Reid snickered. "It'll be a while before anyone knows she's missing, I think."

Peter realized with horror they weren't talking about Dorothy James. They were talking about Tunie!

"Where is she?" Detective Shade asked.

"With the other, tied up in the shipping building."

"And the boy?"

"We're watching his house. He hasn't left it yet. I scraped the girl's initials from the crime scene, so there's no proof there anymore, even if he blabs. If he doesn't leave, I figure I'll break into their place tonight and grab him."

Peter clutched WindUp with damp palms. Detective Shade was involved. They knew where Peter lived. They were coming after him!

"I don't like this. It's gotten way out of hand," Detective Shade snapped. "Now we've got to figure out what to do with *three* kids, instead of just the one. And these last two ain't worth squat!"

Reid laughed nastily. "Don't blow your wig. That only makes them easier to deal with. We sneak 'em out on a boat, and over they go. No bodies, no proof."

In the bushes, Peter swallowed. Reid had called Detective Shade "Peg Leg." The tapping sound Horus had heard . . . Peter realized that must have been Detective Shade walking. Shade had been the other person in the tent at the fair. He'd helped kidnap Dorothy James!

Peter heard fingers drumming on a desk. Shade said, "Nobody's drowning anybody, but the sooner we scram, the better. We need to move up our timeline. Get in touch with James. Tell him if he doesn't sign over the paperwork for those ships today, his daughter, Dorothy, gets the kiss-off."

Reid cleared his throat. "Let's say I do. What's to keep him from grabbing us and taking back those ships the minute he has his daughter?"

Shade laughed. "Oh, we'll be halfway to our smuggling friends in the Caribbean by that time. We'll sell 'em those ships and spend the rest of our lives counting our cabbage in a tropical paradise. They can't catch us if we never come back!"

Reid snickered along. "I've got some packing to do, then."

Another slurping sound came through WindUp's speaker.

"How can you drink this garbage water?" Reid complained.

"Hey, don't pour that on my plant, you egg!" Shade said.

Then Peter heard Reid say suspiciously, "What's this?"

There was a rattling sound, and Peter realized Reid had discovered the intercom device in Shade's office. Reid was pulling it from the plant!

Reid's nasal voice was harsh. "Is this yours? Are you snoopin'?" He raised his voice in accusation. "Are you some kind of GI man, recordin' me?"

"Hush!" Shade said sharply. "It ain't mine, genius. Let me see it."

In Peter's hands, WindUp began to emit a high-pitched shriek. It was feedback—they must have moved closer to the window, and the intercom and WindUp were interfering with each other! The sound was noticeably loud. It would draw their attention for sure! Peter started to scoot out from under the bush, but his shirt snagged on a branch. He heard the window behind him open, and two large, bony hands yanked him up off the ground. As quickly as he could, Peter threw WindUp over the bush.

"Help!" Peter shouted, but Reid pulled him roughly through the window. Peter struggled, knocking his head on the sash. Reid clamped a cloth dampened with some kind of chemical over Peter's mouth. Peter drew in a deep breath and blacked out instantly.

CHAPTER 25

Tunie blinked. The sideways world looked blurry, like smeared paint, and the overwhelming smell of hickory was nauseating. She swallowed, and her tongue felt strange, thick and dry like a stuffed sock.

"Here," came a girl's voice. "Drink some water. It helps."

Tunie blinked again and struggled up to a sitting position. She was on a plank floor in a stifling, dim room with a steeply angled roof. Her ankles and wrists were bound with rope. Beside her was a girl in a tattered blue dress, similarly bound, holding a metal cup of water in her hands. Tunie recognized her from the pictures on the MISSING posters around town, and from the descriptions she and Peter had read a hundred times. She was Dorothy James.

Tunie accepted the cup. She tried to say, "Thanks," but it came out a whisper. She drank the tin-flavored water gratefully. She kept blinking, and the edges of the shapes around her began to sharpen. A low groan drew her attention to a huddled mass on the floor near the door.

"He's alive, at least," Dorothy James whispered, "but the back of his head is hurt. I tried to wash it off a moment ago, and it woke him up a little."

"Peter?" Tunie managed, coughing. "Peter! Is that you?"

Tunie scooted along the rough wooden floor toward her friend, dragging herself forward with her heels. It was definitely Peter, pale but breathing. He was lying in a puddle of rose-tinted water. Tunie looked around for WindUp or Peter's knapsack, but he was empty-handed.

"Peter! Are you okay? Can you hear me?" Tunie was trying her best not to cry.

Peter's eyes fluttered open.

"Ow, my head," he said weakly.

Tunie let out the breath she hadn't realized she was holding. "Can you sit up? Do you want some water?"

Peter nodded and winced.

Dorothy scooted over to help. Between the two of them, they were able to get Peter to sit up against the wall and sip some water. He stared at Dorothy, taking in her brown hair, her eyes.

"You're here," he said to Dorothy croakily. "We've been searching."

Dorothy looked dismayed. "Thanks, but I think finding me meant finding trouble."

"Where are we?" Peter asked over the rim of the tin cup.

Tunie took a calming breath and glanced around.

"From the hickory smell, I'm guessing we're in or near that shipping building, the one where we first saw the mustached man," Tunie said.

"His name is Curtis Reid," Peter told her. "He's the one who caught me."

Tunie wasn't surprised.

"He grabbed me from the museum, too. I was looking for Horus, and he knocked me out with a rag soaked in some kind of smelly stuff."

Dorothy nodded. "I think it was chloroform. One of them said he had to knock you both out again to make sure you were quiet on the way here. They brought you both up after lunchtime, and you've been out for hours. That's what he did to me at the fair. He had help, another man."

Peter said, "A police officer with a wooden leg?"

Dorothy's voice rose with surprise. "Yes! How did you know?"

"Wait," Tunie said, slowly taking in Peter's comment. "What do you mean, the other man was a police officer?"

Peter said, "I hid outside Detective Shade's office

today and overheard Shade and Reid making a plan. Remember the tapping sound Horus heard? That was Shade's peg leg rapping when he walked. He had it covered up with a shoe yesterday, so we didn't see it. Detective Shade has been working with Reid all along, trying to get Dorothy's father to sign over some ships."

Dorothy spoke up. "My father already signed over one ship, but then Shade and Reid said if it was that easy, they wanted more. It won't be simple for my father to arrange. It's a partnership—those ships aren't his alone."

Peter told them about how Shade planned to pressure Dorothy's father to sign over the ships today.

"We've made them anxious, so now they're in a hurry," Peter said. He looked a little less pale. "They plan to sail them down to the Caribbean and sell them to smugglers. They figure they'll get rich and never come back."

It took a moment for all of this to sink in. Detective Shade was the only police officer they'd talked to in detail about Dorothy. Tunie hadn't told her father anything. She'd left a note saying she was going to the museum.

"Did you tell your dad about the headband or the message on the roof or anything?" Tunie asked Peter.

He shook his head, angrily tugging at the rope binding his hands.

"This is a catastrophe. We took our information to the one person we shouldn't have! Nobody would have missed me for a while, either. My family thought I was in the cellar doing inventory all day," Peter said miserably.

Tunie realized that Shade and Reid would not be able to hold either of them ransom for anything valuable.

"What will they do to us?" She felt sick. "We know too much."

Peter gave up on the rope. "I don't know."

"We need to get out of here." Tunie spotted an under-sized square window on the far wall. Whitish light was filtering into the room through its dirty pane. The window was much too small for any of them to crawl out, and anyway, she suspected they were fairly high up off the ground; they seemed to be in an attic, judging from the triangular roof around them. Tunie slid over to the wall and lurched awkwardly to her feet. Standing on her tiptoes, she could just see over the edge of the sill.

Far below, she saw the docks, and people moving around. They looked like ants, unloading cargo from a huge metal ship and carrying crates to carts. It was growing late—already the sun was low on the horizon. The building Tunie and the others were in stood only three stories tall, but it was set into the side of a fairly steep hill; even if she shouted at the top of her lungs, nobody down there would hear her. She managed to crack the window open a tiny bit, and a swirl of cooler air touched her perspiring forehead.

Tunie stopped craning to see out the window and started surveying the room instead.

Dorothy said, "There's nothing here. Believe me, I've searched every nook and cranny of this place. I thought if I could find a loose nail, I could use it to get these ropes off my arms. They chafe."

Indeed, Dorothy's bindings had scraped against the skin around them, leaving her forearms red and irritated. Tunie felt sorry for Dorothy, and terribly guilty that she'd begun the search for Dorothy in earnest only because of the reward. She would have bet anything that Peter felt the same way.

Tunie took in Dorothy's tangled hair and filthy clothes. The pale blue dress matched the headband Perch had found.

"Have they kept you up here the whole time?" Tunie asked Dorothy.

Dorothy nodded. "I'd give anything to get out of here," she said in a choked voice, then laughed, "and into a bath!"

Tunie felt genuine admiration, watching Dorothy try to make light of their situation. She was tough.

"Let's see if there's any way out," Peter said. "Maybe new eyes will turn something up."

Dorothy, Peter, and Tunie spread out and went over every inch of the space, but it seemed their captors had left nothing to chance. The room was enclosed, and solid. Even the glass in the window was extremely thick, and they had nothing they could use to smash it.

They stopped for a water break. Tunie's stomach was

growling audibly. She tried to ignore it. Suddenly a dark shape flew into the room and circled over their heads, flapping. Dorothy shrieked, but Tunie gave a cry of joy.

"Perch! You found us!"

The bat swooped down and landed on Tunie's arm. She smiled tearfully at her furry friend.

"I'm so glad to see you!" Tunie said. Perch tilted his head and piped comfortingly.

"That's Tunie's pet bat, Perch," Peter explained to Dorothy, perking up. "He's quite intelligent."

Perch preened and gave a businesslike shrill.

"Let's see," Tunie said. "If you can find something to cut these ropes, that would be a great help! A paper and pen would be good, too, so we can send a message to our parents, or Officer Hill."

Perch squeaked and took off through the small open window.

"Be quick, Perch!" Tunie called after him. The kidnappers could return at any moment. Who knew how much time was left?

As if in answer to Tunie's fears, she heard the loud, low wail of a boat horn approaching.

CHAPTER 26

The waiting. The waiting was torture. Horus wished he could drum his bony fingers, tap his wrapped metatarsals, anything to relieve some of this nervous energy building inside him. He'd been waiting for the sun to set for what seemed like an eternity—and nobody knew an eternity like Horus. Museum visitors came and went, peering and murmuring, laughing and talking, oblivious to the evil that was going on in their own town. Finally the crowds thinned, dwindling to the last few onlookers, and then there was the wonderful silence when the buzzing lights switched off.

Trying to move before the curse fully allowed it was like trying to walk through a giant tank of jam. Horus attempted to sit up again and again, only to feel that invisible drag. Finally he was able to struggle upright.

He clambered over the stone edge of his sarcophagus, bandages rasping. Then he fished around for the drawing he'd made of the kidnapper. He stood still in the echoing exhibit, paper in hand.

"Now what?" Horus said aloud. He'd think better with his sling stone. He ran to the kitchen, grabbed the frying pan, and hurried to smash the glass case. He took out the stone. With its familiar weight in his hand, he considered what to do.

He could try to get the attention of the night watchman, George. The man was Tunie's neighbor, she'd said. If he knew Tunie, he was likely to help. The problem was, Horus had never successfully gotten the man's attention before. The watchman had walked right past Horus as the mummy sat on the floor, directly in George's path, drinking tea, and George never seemed to see or hear a thing. He never responded to the nightly shattering of the sling stone case. Horus had even tried having conversations with the man, on the time or two he'd had cause to come by the exhibit. George never noticed anything.

Well, Horus had to try. He returned to the small kitchen area and found a large serving spoon and a metal bowl. He carried them over to the door near the hallway and started banging on the bowl with the spoon.

Clang! Clang! Cling! Clang!

Horus winced at every earsplitting whack, but after twenty minutes there was no sign of the watchman. Every minute that passed was another minute Tunie was in the hands of that vile man. Horus blinked sepia tears from his eyes, setting the bowl and spoon on the floor and picking up the sketch and his stone.

He peered through the small window in the doorway to the hall. George was up the stairs. Horus need only go down the hall and up the stairs to find him.

Just the thought of opening the door made Horus tremble. He knew what would happen. One never forgot that kind of pain. He had to do it, though, and not just because Tunie had brought him books. He had to do it because he'd been a bad boy when he'd lived, and a bad mummy afterward, and here, finally, was his chance to be good. He had to do it for all the people he'd hurt before. Most especially, he had to do it because he cared about her. He had to do it for Tunie.

His small, bandaged hand reached for the doorknob.

"Kindness travels," he whispered. Then: "For Tunie!"

Saying it aloud made him feel braver, so he said it again. "For Tunie!"

He shouted it as he flung open the door.

"For Tunie!" He shouldered his way through, and instantly the pain licked up his calves, the soles of his feet searing with each step down the tile hallway. He gripped the carved stone and the drawing.

"FOR TUNIE!" Horus cried as the burning sensation traveled up his spine and down each of his arms. He staggered to the stairwell.

"FOR . . . TUNIE!" the frail little mummy shouted.

As he rose up each step, his entire body shivered with pain.

"FOR! TUNIE!" he shrieked. By the time he reached the top of the stairs, Horus could no longer walk. He fell to his knees and crawled into George's office. Horus's vision was beginning to dim, and dense flocks of black dots obscured his vision. He felt like his whole skeleton was on fire. Through the haze of pain, Horus made out the bulk of the night watchman at his desk, his back to the door through which Horus dragged himself.

"FOR . . . TUNIE . . . ," Horus gasped out one last time. He reached up and slammed the drawing onto the watchman's desk. He'd done it! He'd defied the curse! Tunie had a chance! It was Horus's last thought before, at last, the pain of the curse overwhelmed him, and he collapsed to the floor.

CHAPTER 27

George's chair creaked as he turned his head slightly to one side.

"What's this?" he said, reaching for the paper on his desk. "Where did this come from?"

He looked over the pen drawing—a quite good one, really—and a feeling of dread fell over him. He read the accompanying note.

Who could have written this? Was it a joke? He'd heard Tunie come in at the end of his last shift, in the early morning. She hadn't come in this evening, though—she always made a point of calling up to George when she did.

George decided to make sure she wasn't in the museum. He descended the stairs and checked every exhibit.

"Tunie?" he called. His voice sounded hollow in the tiled rooms.

After making certain Tunie was not around, George returned to his office. He reached for the phone and dialed the police.

A gruff man's voice answered. "Harbortown Police Station, Officer Hill speaking. What's your emergency?"

George cleared his throat. "I think I need to report a kidnapping."

He described the man to Officer Hill, who arranged for an officer to come by the museum right away and pick up the drawing. Speaking to the policeman made George feel more anxious. Tunie could be in real danger.

"You've got to find her," George said to the police officer on the line, thinking of the earnest girl who was always looking out for him and his mother, not to mention her own sick father.

"Tunie's a friend," Officer Hill said through the receiver. "I'd do anything for Tunie."

For Tunie, George thought as he hung up the phone. Now why did those words seem to be hovering in the air?

CHAPTER 28

"This is useless," Tunie said. The tips of her fingers were chafed red from pulling at the rope around Dorothy's wrists. "The knots are just too tight."

Peter spit out tiny fibers onto the floor. He'd been chewing at his bonds, with discouraging results.

"I'm only making these soggy."

There wasn't much else to do.

After a long stretch, Perch finally flitted into the attic through the small square window. He dropped his treasures into Tunie's hands: a nail file, a pen, and a scrap of paper.

"Perch," Tunie said, smiling, with tears in her eyes. "You are a most exceptional bat."

Dorothy was watching Perch with wonder.

"That's an understatement," she said.

Peter laughed. "Nice work, Perch."

Perch landed on a rafter and strutted, upside down, looking quite satisfied. Tunie handed the file to Dorothy.

"You and Peter try to cut through each other's ropes. I'll write a note for Perch to deliver to Officer Hill."

"Okeydokey." Dorothy accepted the file and scooted over near Peter. She began sawing away at the ropes binding his hands. Tunie thought that for someone who could have been a delicate, pampered girl, Dorothy was surprisingly tough. If they got out of this mess, they might even be friends.

Tunie did the best she could with her hands bound tightly together. Her fingers cramped from holding the pen at an uncomfortable slant, and lettering was arduous and slow. She was aware of every passing moment as she wrote out their situation.

> Dear Officer Hill,
>   Peter Bartholomew, Dorothy James, and I are being held captive in the attic of Billowing Sails Shipping on Franklin Street, near the harbor.

All at once she heard clumping and indistinguishable voices drawing near. Tunie rushed to jot down as much as she could.

> Detective Shade and a man named Curtis R

Before she could finish, the trapdoor flung open with a bang. She stuffed the pen and paper into her sock, and saw Peter do the same with the metal file.

Reid's greasy head appeared first, followed by his lanky frame. He held handkerchiefs in his hands. Detective Shade followed him up the ladder.

Detective Shade eyed them coldly with his close-set eyes, while Reid stuffed a rag in Peter's mouth and secured it with a handkerchief.

Detective Shade spoke sternly. "We're moving you out of here. These gags ought to keep you quiet, but if you get any ideas—if you decide, for example, to make knocking sounds with your knuckles or something of that nature—I will make you quiet, permanently." He looked over at the open window. "What's that doing open?"

Dorothy answered. "It's hot in here. I just wanted some air."

Shade strode over and slammed the window shut.

Oh no! Tunie thought. *Now Perch is stuck in here!* She looked at Peter, but he had his eyes cast down.

Reid gagged Tunie and Dorothy. Then he and Shade hauled Peter away. The ropes around his ankles made descending the ladder impossible, so they slung Peter around like a sack of flour. Tunie prayed they wouldn't notice the half-sawed ropes around his wrists.

While the two men were busy carrying Peter downstairs, Tunie pulled the crumpled note out of her sock, and Perch swooped down and snatched it in his tiny claws, flying rapidly back up to the ceiling and disappearing behind an exposed wooden beam.

The men returned and carried Dorothy away.

Maybe they would leave the attic entrance open, and Perch could fly out that way, Tunie hoped. Alas, when Shade and Reid carried her down, Reid reached up and pulled the trapdoor shut behind them.

Perch was trapped.

Hanging upside down over Reid's shoulder, Tunie spied three large black traveling trunks on the floor: two closed, one ajar. Tunie just had time to read the words stenciled on the open trunk—LIVE CARGO—and see the breathing holes punched in its sides before Reid and Shade dropped her inside it roughly.

She could see a little bit of the wall through the breathing hole closest to her face. She tried to pull the gag from her mouth, but it was too tight, and she couldn't reach behind her head in the tight quarters. Suddenly the box lurched up, and Tunie felt she was being carried. She bumped and jostled along for several minutes, feeling cool air that smelled of the ocean coming in through the small holes. Then up, up, up. Finally her trunk landed with a thud. She heard voices and a seagull squawking. She was moving up and down gently. Rocking. She was on a boat.

Poor Perch was locked in the attic, Tunie thought despairingly. Her father and Peter's parents didn't know where they were. Horus was the only one who had a clue what was happening, and he couldn't communicate with anyone! Even if Perch somehow managed to get out and take that note to Officer Hill, they were no longer in the attic where she'd said. She hadn't even signed her name. The police weren't aware Detective Shade was involved in Dorothy's kidnapping.

There was no way anyone would find them.

CHAPTER 29

Officer Hill took one look at the sketch his colleague had brought in from the museum—the drawing showed a curled mustache, a narrow face—and recognized him.

"This fellow was in to see Detective Shade earlier today!" Officer Hill said to his partner, Officer Lovejoy. Hill shook his head admiringly. "Shade must be onto him. I bet he called this phony in for questioning. Let's show Shade the sketch."

Hill and Lovejoy hurried to Detective Shade's office and were surprised to find it empty.

Officer Hill frowned. "That's odd. These are his office hours." He turned to Lovejoy. "Well, let's see if we can track down this rat ourselves."

They returned to the front desk, and Officer Hill showed the sketch to the gray-haired attendant.

"Doris, this man came in to see Detective Shade today. I don't suppose you caught his name?"

Doris looked at the sketch over the top of her bifocals. "I remember him. Curtis Reid. Detective Shade told me to send him on back to his office when he arrived."

"Terrific," said Officer Hill. "Can you get on the horn to the post office? Let's see if we can get an address for Curtis Reid."

"You got it." Doris lifted the receiver.

A familiar, disheveled-looking man wearing spectacles and holding a toy robot shoved open the station door.

"Sir," the man said to Officer Hill a little wildly, "I believe my son might be missing." He straightened his glasses, which were slipping off his nose. "He was meant to be in the house all day, but he snuck out and we can't find him. I've been searching for hours. I came to see if anyone had reported seeing him, and I found this right outside—this is his favorite robot, WindUp. Peter would never leave him anywhere! I know it sounds trivial, but I'm very worried."

Officer Hill came forward to show him a seat.

"I remember you, Mr. Bartholomew, and your son, Peter. Something is going on. We believe Peter's friend Tunie has been kidnapped," Officer Hill said.

"Kidnapped?" Mr. Bartholomew grew pale and sank down into the chair, clutching the robot. "Why? Could Peter have been with her? Does it have something to do with the mugging they witnessed last night?"

"Mugging?" Officer Hill blinked. "Sir, they came in with information about the kidnapper in the Dorothy James case."

Mr. Bartholomew looked baffled. "The Dorothy James case? My son said nothing about that. He said they'd seen a mugger attack an old man."

This didn't add up. Why would the boy lie?

"We'll figure out why he told you that. Right now we have a lead on the kidnapper." Officer Hill placed a hand on Mr. Bartholomew's shoulder. "We're following up on it now. You can wait here if you like."

"Yes," Peter's father said. He sat tensely in the chair. "I can't leave until I know Peter's safe."

Meanwhile, Doris was jotting down an address on a notepad, the receiver tucked under her ear. "Down by the wharf, you say? Billowing Sails Shipping? Got it. Thanks, Randy."

She hung up the phone and handed the address to Officer Hill. "He lives down near the wharf, in a room above Billowing Sails Shipping, Inc. Here's the street address."

"Right," said Officer Hill, all business. "Lovejoy and I will head out. Doris, call a couple patrol cars down to the wharf, would you?"

In a lower voice, so that Peter's father wouldn't hear, Hill said grimly, "Let's hope we're not too late to save those kids."

CHAPTER 30

Horus blinked his golden eyes. The unfamiliar ceiling wavered, as if underwater. He carefully sat up, bandages crinkling, and looked around.

"Why, I'm in that fellow George's office on the second floor!" Horus said with excitement. "I'm still here and—and it doesn't hurt!"

The mummy gave a tiny hop, and that felt so good he did a little twirl. Delighted, Horus stood up and began surveying the shelves, touching a clock, a framed photo, a stapler. So many new things! He spied a note stuck to the window of the door. He pulled it off and flipped it over.

"Back in 20 minutes," it read.

Then Horus remembered what had happened.

Tunie'd been kidnapped. . . . Had the night watchman left to find her? Or was he off to see the police? Horus scanned the neat desk. The sketch was gone. Horus was standing here, so obviously he'd accomplished his task.

Then he thought of something else. "Am I trapped here now? In this little space?"

The urge to dance drained away. The exhibit was cavernous compared with this narrow room. It was hardly bigger than a closet. Would this be his new prison? There was only one way to find out.

Horus took a step toward the door and reached for the dull metal knob. He took a deep, unnecessary breath and yanked the door open. Cautiously he placed one small, bandaged foot over the threshold.

Nothing.

Horus gingerly stepped out into the hallway.

Nothing.

"Skittering scarabs!" Horus shouted. "I'm free! Am I free? I might be . . . free!"

He skipped down the hallway linoleum. He sprinted and skidded back and forth for joy on his little stick legs. Then, at the end of the dim hall, he spied the night watchman, George, returning to his office.

"George!" Horus called. He pattered down the hallway to the lit office. He could hear a phone ringing inside.

George answered.

"Mm-hmm. Yes. Billowing Sails Shipping. I've heard of it," said George. He sat down in his desk chair. "No, no, I won't go after them. No, I certainly won't do anything rash. Thanks for letting me know."

George set the receiver back on its hook and stood staring into space.

Horus danced around before him. "Is that where Tunie and Peter are? Go after them! What if the police need help? Go! You must go!"

George didn't seem to see Horus, but he muttered to himself, "What if the police need help?" He pushed back his chair and got to his feet. "It's Tunie, after all. I must go."

George hastily left his office, and Horus padded after him.

The front entrance to the museum was one of the few doors locked with a dead bolt from the inside. George fumbled for his keys, giving Horus time to become nervous and exhilarated. Would he be able to leave the building? What was happening to his curse?

Finally, with a clink of metal on metal, George found the key on the circular ring and opened the door.

Outside, the evening was warm but breezy. The streetlamps glowed, and the stars overhead glimmered. Horus, who had not seen the sky in thousands of years, was struck silent. Those twinkling, everlasting lights, and his old friend, the moon, were still there. He inhaled the fresh air and the smell of trees and grass. A rush of feeling rose in his chest, a tremendous, nameless emotion, as strong and untouchable as a storm.

George descended the steps at a clip.

Horus followed, his feet on the concrete still warm from the day's sun, and walked out into the night.

CHAPTER 31

Good grief. Was this dull file really the best the bat could find?
Inside the trunk, Peter was dripping sweat from the effort of sawing his bindings one-handed at an awkward angle. It had taken ages to cut the rope down to just a strand or two. Peter tugged with all his might, and his hands came free with a snap.

Finally! He plucked away the rope and rubbed at his chafed wrists. Then he immediately pulled the gag from his mouth. His lips and tongue felt unspeakably dry. He swallowed as best he could.

Now for the feet.

To reach his ankles, he had to press his face up against the perforated side of the trunk. The box was rocking back and forth, making things difficult. He sweated all the more, his stomach and back muscles trembling as his fingers worked at the unseen knots. Done!

And now to get himself out.

The trunk was locked, but loosely. The lid opened a crack. Peter slid the file into the gap and pried until he heard something snap. He shoved open the lid, struggled out, and landed with a thud. He was on the deck of a large ship. Peter looked around. The boat was big enough that three train cars would have fit on it, end to end. He could see the moon shining on the water below. Suddenly the whole craft lurched, and Peter grabbed the railing to keep from falling.

Footsteps thudded along the deck, the sailors calling to one another. Peter saw, with dismay, why the boat had pitched like that.

It was pulling away from the dock.

There were about ten men working on the deck by the glow of lanterns and the stars. Peter saw movement and lights on the receding dock. He and the others had been stashed in the shadows, away from the rest of the cargo. He heard Reid's distinctive voice calling out now and then.

Peter crouched beside one of the other trunks.

"Tunie?" he whispered, before realizing she and Dorothy were gagged and unable to respond. He saw the shine of an eye pressed up against an airhole, and instantly got to work.

Using the file, Peter picked the lock in record time,

then glanced around. So far no one had noticed him. He lifted the lid, and Dorothy sat up. He pulled the gag from her mouth. She took a deep breath and mouthed a thank-you to Peter. He loosened the knots at her wrists and feet. As she pulled the ropes off, Peter located Tunie.

Soon all three were free.

"Should we scream?" Tunie whispered. "How do we know if these men are working with Shade and Reid?"

Dorothy was already filling her trunk with sacks of sand stacked nearby. Peter and Tunie looked at her, surprised.

Dorothy whispered urgently.

"The longer they think we're in here, the more time we have to escape," she said.

Peter and Tunie nodded and followed suit. As soon as they'd filled the trunks, Peter, Tunie, and Dorothy crept away, keeping to the shadows. They ducked down and ran as quietly as they could to the other side of the boat.

Peter whispered to Tunie and Dorothy that the boat had just left the harbor.

"We should swim for it," he whispered.

"I think we can make it," Dorothy agreed. "Let's jump!"

Tunie's face fell. "I don't know how to swim," she said. She surveyed the deck. "You two go. It will be easier for just one of us to hide anyway. Then you can send help."

Dorothy and Peter looked at each other.

They were getting farther from the dock with every passing second. Peter had to make a decision.

"Okay. We'll go. Quick, take your shoes off, Dorothy!" He and Dorothy pulled off their shoes and threw them inside a giant coil of rope. Tunie climbed into another and tucked herself down into the dark.

Peter peered at Tunie over the coil's edge.

"I hate to leave you here," Peter said, "but we'll bring help. I promise."

Tunie nodded, looking resolute. "Go! I'll be fine."

Then Dorothy and Peter ran to the ship's rail, climbed up, and leaped overboard.

The sensation of falling lasted only a moment, and then the cold water closed over Peter's head. He swam upward, toward the moon, and took a breath when he emerged. The saltwater stung his chafed wrists. The massive shadow of the ship passed to his left. He spied Dorothy, already swimming for the dock. Peter set to it, too, with strong strokes, not looking back. He would make it to shore. More than his life depended on it.

CHAPTER 32

Officers Hill and Lovejoy knocked on the door of Billowing Sails Shipping, Inc. When no one answered, they let themselves in through the sagging doorframe.

"Curtis Reid? Dorothy? Tunie?" Officer Hill called, stepping into the dark room. "Peter, are you in here?"

He and Lovejoy turned on the lights and searched through the ratty offices on the first floor and the shabby apartment on the second floor, from the threadbare carpets to the water-stained ceilings. There was no sign of Reid or the kidnapped children.

Officer Hill looked around.

"There's another floor above this one. Let's look for access," he said to Lovejoy. They searched high and low until they found a trapdoor above a gloomy servants' staircase at the back of the building. Officer Hill climbed up the ladder first, with Lovejoy close behind him. As he entered the room and looked around, holding his lantern high, a dark shape flitted near his head and a sheet of paper came sailing down from the rafters. It fell at Officer Hill's feet. He bent down and picked it up.

"Why, it's a note—to *me!*" Officer Hill exclaimed.

Lovejoy hurried over and stood beside him. Reading over Hill's shoulder, Lovejoy whistled.

"Look at that fancy handwriting! Fine work, that is. Did a lady write it?" Lovejoy asked.

Officer Hill squinted.

"It's not signed. Looks like the writer was interrupted. She mentions Detective Shade and a Curtis R. That'd be Reid, of course," he said. He thought about the boy, Peter, telling his father he'd seen a mugging, instead of mentioning the Dorothy James case. Could Shade have influenced him?

"The way she mentions Shade *and* Reid . . . do you think Shade could be involved?"

"I do," said Lovejoy sourly.

"Well, yes, actually, it isn't so hard to believe, is it," Officer Hill agreed. "Weaselly fellow. Can't leap to conclusions, I suppose."

But he had his suspicions.

A quick search of the attic showed that the children were no longer there.

"This note could be from Tunie Webster," said Officer

Hill. "She's associated with the two missing kids mentioned here. They might still be nearby. Let's get more men down here. We'll search the harbor. If Reid knows we're onto him, I bet he'll make a run for it. Or a sail for it."

The men did not see Perch dart through the open trapdoor and fly down the stairs, making his way out into the night. They did not see George, the night watchman, follow them down the path to the harbor, nor did they see at his side the small, determined mummy with the brightly gleaming eyes.

CHAPTER 33

On the ship they'd ransomed from Dorothy James's father, Reid paced back and forth in the cramped captain's quarters, while Detective Shade sat nearby, brooding. Finally Shade snapped.

"Look, he signed over this ship, right? It'll be fine. Now would you stop ranging back and forth like a mad hyena and let me think?" What a half portion this Mr. Curtis Reid was, Shade thought, and mean to boot. A few minutes earlier, while Reid was using the toilet, Shade had found a wicked-looking knife in the coat Reid left behind. Shade hid the knife and replaced it with a banana, to make sure Reid didn't do anything stupid. Once they were in the Caribbean, he'd find a way to get rid of the man.

Reid stopped and glared.

"You said you'd keep this contained," Reid snarled at Shade, jabbing a finger at the air in his direction. "But that was a copper we saw pulling up at the shipping company, you wet sock."

Shade rubbed his hands over his face. "We have a head start. We'll take one of those routes through rough waters to save time. They won't follow us there."

Reid stared at him with his narrow eyes. "With the man's daughter on board? You're wacky. He won't stop until he has her back!"

Shade exhaled. The numskull had a point. "You're right, you're right." He tapped a pen on the desk as he thought. "So we put our plan into effect a little earlier than we thought—using her as a decoy. Go set her off in a lifeboat with a torch. They'll sooner go after the girl than us, dig?"

Reid nodded. "All right. What about the other two?"

Shade waved a dismissive hand. "Lock 'em in the hold, now that the men are done loading. We'll ditch them once we get there."

"Right." Reid pulled on his coat and strode on his long legs to the door. He looked over his shoulder at Shade, who was leaning back in his seat. "Come on, then, shake a leg. I ain't doing this on my own."

Reluctantly, Shade got to his feet—or foot. He'd removed the boot, and he followed Reid with a rap-rap-rapping of his peg leg to the shadowy nook where they'd stashed the trunks. Shade was a bit unsteady. He put a hand out to keep himself from falling over on the rolling deck.

"The one marked *fragile* holds the James girl," Shade whispered.

Reid stooped to the trunk.

"That you, Dorothy?" he said.

Detective Shade shushed him. "Don't draw attention! They can't answer you anyway. They're gagged, you twit. Help me carry this over to the lifeboat."

The turning of the ship changed the position of the moon, and it lit up their part of the ship.

He and Shade each took one end of the trunk.

Reid shook his head. "Shouldn't have bothered with these special containers," he grumbled. "One without airholes would have done away with the kids. Then we wouldn't have to worry about 'em."

"What's wrong with you? We're no murderers."

They lowered the trunk to the deck with a thud. Shade opened it, expecting to find Dorothy bound and gagged. Instead, he discovered the bags of ballast the children had left behind. The two men stared.

Shade slammed shut the lid of the trunk.

"What have you done now? You've gone and lost her!" He glared accusingly at Reid. "I gave you one thing to do—smuggle the kids on board this ship—and you couldn't even manage that? Is there a brain in your skull at all, or just a little loose gravel rattling around?!"

Reid narrowed his eyes hatefully at Shade.

"Me?" he hissed. "This is all your fault, you grifter. You're trying to get me hanged, is what."

Shade laughed in disbelief. "What are you talking about?"

Reid reached into his coat and pulled out . . . a banana. He glanced at it, perplexed, and then pointed it at Shade.

"How did those kids know I took Dorothy to that rooftop?" Reid shook the banana. "You tipped them off, that's how! No one else could have seen me there, unless they were flying about overhead!"

He advanced on Detective Shade, brandishing the banana. Shade edged to the side, keeping the weighted trunk between them. The wet deck was slippery beneath his wooden peg leg.

Shade held his hands out in a peaceable gesture. "All right, all right, now. Let's calm down and think for a minute."

Reid, however, did not put away the fruit. He kept his dark eyes on Shade.

"Oh, I *am* thinking," Reid said, "and what I'm thinkin' is, you're implementin' your own plan here. You're going to steal the money we make from selling this ship for yourself! Or you'll tell the coppers I was the one who kidnapped Dorothy, and you were trying to stop me! At the very least, you'd skip going to the big house, and you'd get the reward from James. He doesn't know you an' me are the ones holdin' his daughter for ransom, after all."

Shade nearly roared in anger. "You absolute dimwit! I'm not plotting against you! Don't you see the problem is we don't know where the children are?! They'll implicate us both if we don't find them!"

"You're wrong," Reid said. "They won't implicate us both."

He lunged over the trunk and started whapping Shade around the head with the banana. The two men grappled, and Shade took a swing at Reid's jaw but missed. With a kick of one long leg, Reid managed to knock Shade's good foot out from under him. Shade slid on his peg leg, landing half in the open trunk. He struggled to stand, but Reid wrestled him down all the way into the trunk, then slammed the lid and fastened it with the lock.

Shade banged on the wall of the trunk.

He called out, "Without me, you'll lose everything! I'm the one who knows the buyers for this ship! They won't trust you!"

"Quiet, or I'll heave you over!" Reid snarled. "I need to think what I want to do with you."

Shade ceased his thumping and hollering. He peered out through one of the airholes in the trunk.

Reid straightened his clothes. Shade felt him shove the trunk along the deck. Reid leaned down to the airholes.

"One peep out of you and over you go, you understand?"

Shade didn't respond.

"Good," Reid said. He stood as if to leave. Then Shade and Reid heard it. It came from the coils of rope beside Shade's trunk.

There it was again—a muffled, but still audible, *"Ah-choo!"*

CHAPTER 34

Perch soared out over the sea in the humid night air. The ocean was an odd, vast space, the echoes coming back empty, empty, empty. He scanned the undulating surface below him until suddenly: There! A shape below. It was a ship! He knew instantly that Tunie was on board.

There was no time to check on her. Perch swooped like a boomerang, heading back to the docks. He found Officers Hill and Lovejoy questioning dockworkers, and flew down, squeaking his news: he'd found Tunie!

"Argh! Get it away!" Lovejoy swatted at Perch with his officer's hat, nearly knocking Perch out of the sky. Perch landed upside down on a lamppost, squeaking.

"Something wrong with that creature," muttered Hill, eyeing the bat. "Why isn't it flying off? Might have rabies."

Perch squeaked with frustration. How could he communicate with these people? All at once, he spotted a familiar figure, hanging back by a docked ship. His bandages dangled loosely at his elbows, wrists, and knees, and his eyes pierced the inky dark like candle flames. Perch glided over to Horus.

"Why, hullo," Horus said to Perch, who found purchase on a dangling rope. "Are you looking for Tunie, too?"

Excited, Perch squeaked an affirmative.

Horus's eyes glowed. "And you found her?"

Again Perch squeaked, flying toward the water and then back to Horus.

"She's on a boat?" Horus guessed.

Perch nodded.

Horus looked out at the harbor and then tiptoed over to another man Perch hadn't noticed. It was George, their neighbor! Perch flapped nearby. George looked up.

"Oh! Hiya, Perch," George said, glancing at Perch and then turning his attention back to the police.

Horus sidled right up to George and spoke as loudly as he could.

"Tunie is on a boat! We must look for her! Now—before it's too late!"

George frowned.

"These police are taking too long questioning folks," George said quietly to himself. "Tunie's probably out on a boat somewhere."

George looked around and saw an old man sitting in a patchwork dory, getting ready to do some night fishing. He approached the fisherman.

"I'm wondering if I could rent your boat," George said to the whiskery fellow.

The old man, who had only one or two teeth left in his mouth, spit off to the side. "Not fer rent," he said.

"I'll pay you," George said, and named a week's salary. The old man's eyes widened.

"Let's see it," the old man croaked. When he saw the bills, he cackled with glee.

"I'm off to the tavern, then! Bring my boat back safe! I know the police around here if you don't!" the old man threatened, but then scampered off, jolly at the idea of a pint instead of a night's work.

George and Horus climbed on board. Perch flew back and forth from the boat in Tunie's direction.

Horus said loudly, "We should head southwest."

George untied the boat and sat at the oars.

"Southwest, I think," George muttered.

Perch made sure they were headed in the right direction and then flapped off into the night to find Tunie. A tremor of exhaustion shook his wings, and he dropped momentarily before righting himself. The tiny bat felt a rush of anxiety as he fluttered out over the measureless, surging sea.

CHAPTER 35

Another small, unexpected wave slapped Peter roughly in the face. He took in a mouthful or two of seawater and coughed. Beside him, he could hear Dorothy sputtering.

This was not good.

They were both strong swimmers. Using a slow sideways stroke, Peter had caught up with Dorothy, and the two of them had been swimming side by side in the choppy brine for what felt like hours. Peter's arms and legs were growing weary from the exertion of swimming, and his lungs burned. Yet for all his labor, the harbor lights seemed only slightly closer, and a little bit farther east than when they'd started. Were they swimming against a current, or had he misjudged the distance?

Dorothy abruptly stopped swimming. She flipped onto her back, floating and breathing heavily.

"I can't make it," Dorothy said, breathless. "I'm too tired to keep swimming. I'll drown for sure if I keep at it. You go ahead. I'll float here as long as I can," she said. "Send help."

Peter turned over onto his back, too.

"I can't do it, either," Peter said helplessly, staring up at the stars. They looked glittery and powdery to him, like snow. The water lapped at his ears. He reached out his wet fingers and touched Dorothy's hand reassuringly.

Peter thought of how he'd resented this ocean, the insurmountable cost and effort of crossing it, and his mother for choosing to go to its other side. The cure for her disease—the brisk air of the Alps—had not saved her. He wondered if his dad ever felt angry about it, too—that she'd chosen to go there on her own, and left them. He wished he'd discussed it with his father. He'd never have the opportunity now.

"I'm scared," Dorothy whispered.

Peter swallowed. "Me too."

"Nobody knows where we are. We're drifting out to sea. It's nighttime, and there aren't many ships, and even if there were, they'd never see us. They'd run us over!" Dorothy said. She was starting to sound panicked.

Peter could feel himself growing more anxious with every point Dorothy made. It was true. Chances were they'd die out here. He pictured WindUp, lying alone by the shrubbery where Peter had tossed him. His robot would rust in the rain if no one came to get him. Peter shoved the thought away.

"We just have to keep calm," Peter said. "It doesn't take much energy to float. Your dad is going to come after that boat."

"But when?" Dorothy said softly.

"Soon," Peter lied. It made him feel better to say it, so he said it again. "Soon."

CHAPTER 36

Tunie had tried to muffle the sneeze but couldn't. She heard Reid's footsteps stop.

He knew she was there.

Tunie crouched down as far as she could inside the dank, shadowy coil of rope and gripped the file in her fist. Reid was moving quietly now. She could no longer hear his boots treading on the wooden deck.

He was going to find her. She might as well use the element of surprise to her advantage.

She leaped out of the coiled rope and shouted at the top of her lungs, "BAH!"

Reid startled, but a moment later he lunged forward, his hand closing punishingly around her upper arm.

"Where are the other two?" he snarled, shaking Tunie hard.

"They jumped ship," Tunie shot back. "They're swimming to shore right now. The police will be here soon!"

But Reid only laughed wickedly. "Then they did the job for us! They'll never make it to the harbor. The tide's going out—they'll be swept out to sea. Now it's your turn."

He tried to haul Tunie over to the edge of the ship. She gripped the file and jabbed at the man's arm. He howled and let go of Tunie, who turned to flee.

Reid was too quick for her, though. With his uninjured hand, he grabbed hold of Tunie's braids and yanked. Tugged backward, Tunie fell to the deck hard.

"Oof," she said, the air leaving her lungs on impact. The file clattered away across the deck. She managed to stand, but Reid grabbed her from behind, his arms around her in a crushing bear hug. Her arms were pinned to her sides. Tunie thrashed, and the back of her skull connected with Reid's nose in a loud crunch.

"Argh!" he shouted, dropping her and clutching his nose. Tunie spun away.

Then, as she watched, a burlap sack flew through the air and over Reid's head.

Dark wings fluttered around the struggling man.

"Perch!" Tunie cried.

Perch flapped past Tunie, and she ran after him, taking advantage of Reid's brief incapacitation. The bat guided her through a doorway. There was a hatch. Tunie lifted it and spied a ladder that led into darkness. It was a storage hold.

Perch squeaked.

"You lead," Tunie said in a whisper. "Find me a good place to hide!"

She descended the ladder and felt her way among the crates, groping in the darkness.

Perch squeaked now and then, and she followed him through the close maze of cargo. She climbed up a few crates and then between some stacked trunks. Many of the boxes were under nets, tied down, so as not to shift. Tunie fit narrowly between two large, netted stacks.

"Is help coming?" Tunie asked.

Perch squeaked an affirmative.

"So Peter and Dorothy made it!" Tunie whispered, relieved.

Perch made a worried sound.

"They didn't?" Tunie said. "Perch, you have to find them! They were swimming for shore off the side of the boat more than an hour ago. They might be in trouble! Will you look for them? Please?"

Perch gripped her finger with his claws in the dark, as if he didn't want to let her go.

"You've done plenty," Tunie said. "I'll hide here until help comes. Go!"

Perch reluctantly flew away. Tunie realized then that they'd left the hatch open, and with the hatch open, Reid would know where to look for her. The ship's hold was huge but not endless; eventually he'd find her.

Tunie prayed that whatever help was on the way would hurry. She made herself as small as she could and listened. She heard the faint ringing sound of feet on the metal rungs of the ladder, and the sound of someone stepping down into the hold.

CHAPTER 37

Officer Hill knew at once that the handsome, well-dressed man approaching him across the wharf with two uniformed police officers was Christopher James. Officer Hill held out his hand, and Mr. James shook it.

"Long story short," one of the officers said to Hill. "The people who kidnapped Mr. James's daughter demanded one of his steamships as ransom. He gave them the ship and has been waiting at a warehouse for them to bring his daughter in exchange. They didn't show."

"I have a fast yacht at my disposal," Mr. James said immediately, by way of introduction. "An express cruiser."

Officer Hill nodded curtly. "We'll take it. The military is sending a boat, but it might take too long. Men!" He blew his whistle, drawing the attention of the other uniformed officers swarming the lantern-lit dock. "We have a boat! Let's go!"

Within a quarter hour, the sleek wooden cruiser lifted anchor with twenty policemen, ten sailors and a captain, and the shipping magnate Christopher James aboard. The police knew Reid and Shade would be sailing for the mouth of the harbor, if they hadn't made it there yet. Mr. James insisted on remaining on deck, a spyglass to his eye. He scanned the water again and again.

"There are fewer ships out here these days—we're exporting half as much as we were before 1929. We can thank the Depression for that. The ship they're on is a freight steamer, painted black," Mr. James said. "The smokestack has four bands of color: yellow, red, white, blue. I'll know it when I see it."

Officer Hill took in the man's elegant double-breasted suit, his scattered, anxious air, and his weary aspect. In one fist, he tightly gripped a blue pocket kerchief, worrying the material between his thumb and forefinger.

"We'll find her, sir," Officer Hill said reassuringly.

Mr. James did not take his eyes off the horizon.

"I should have come to you. I should have contacted the police right away; I see that now," Mr. James said hoarsely. "But they threatened her. My little Dorothy. I couldn't even tell my wife. They said they had a man on the inside, and they'd know the moment I contacted the police."

"Is that so? It might be Detective Dedrick Shade," Officer Hill said. "He may be in league with a man named Curtis Reid. Two other children are missing along with Dorothy. Believe me when I say we'll find out the truth about this, and whoever is responsible will pay."

"There! That painted smokestack!" Mr. James pointed it out to the captain. "It's definitely my ship."

"I see it," the captain said.

The yacht swerved beneath their feet as the captain altered its course.

They were almost there.

CHAPTER 38

It had been a great and terrible night. Horus breathed in the fishy salt air. He marveled at the stars and the moonglow, the slapping waves, the temperate breeze sifting through his linen wraps. He admired the gentle rocking motion of the boat, and the miracle of the sheer space around him, the endless space!

As he tilted his head up once more, he spied Perch, blacking out the stars as he flapped toward their little boat.

George ducked at first, but when Perch landed softly in the boat, he took a closer look. "Perch! We must be going the right way!" George exclaimed happily.

Perch let out a series of screeches that let Horus know something was wrong.

Horus touched the bat softly.

"Do we need to change course?" Horus asked.

Perch squeaked and indicated a direction. The little bat looked exhausted. His wings were drooping.

Horus spoke loudly, using his influence over George to adjust their course. "Head westerly. The children are in trouble."

George frowned, and rowed with one oar, moving the boat a little more to the west. He was breathing hard with the effort of rowing, but in this direction, the little dory caught a current, and their pace quickened.

The smack of the water against the boat's wooden sides and the dip of the oars in the ocean were the only sounds as the night watchman, the mummy, and the bat headed out on the great expanse of water.

Horus peered through the darkness and spied, at a distance, two pale figures in the water. They vanished behind a wave and reappeared, bobbing on the surface.

"That way, George!" Horus said urgently, clutching the boat's edge. "Faster, faster!"

George, suddenly inspired to row even harder, bent over the oars.

They were close now. As Horus watched the two people, one of them slid away, disappearing under the water.

"No!" Horus shouted, leaning out over the shadowy water. He waited. Whoever it was did not resurface.

Without pausing to think, Horus dove into the warm, salty sea.

The liquid tugged at his wraps as Horus swam

underwater, keeping his eye on the dropping figure, floating downward to the dark ocean floor. The person wore a dress that billowed out in a bell shape. A girl. He could almost reach her. The mummy kicked his small, bony feet. It was difficult to swim holding on to the sling stone. He hesitated for a moment—out here, he might lose it forever. And then he dropped it. The rock sank into the murk and vanished. Horus cupped his skeletal hands and moved his ancient arms as fast as he could.

He had to get to her.

CHAPTER 39

Dorothy slid away under the water so silently that it took Peter a moment to notice. He'd been keeping his eyes turned toward the sky, to keep the water off his face as well as he could. When her fingers drifted away from his, it took him a few seconds to look over to where she'd been.

Dorothy was gone.

Frantic, Peter began treading water, looking around beneath the surface, but though the moon was bright, it was difficult to see at all.

"Dorothy!" he called. He took a great breath and went underwater, peering through the gloom, the salt stinging his eyes. He saw nothing.

He broke through the surface, gasping for air, and

tried again. He swam as deep as he dared, but soon his lungs were burning, and his body was tired, too tired.

Peter used all his energy to swim up to the surface, and as he took in a great breath, he was nearly struck by a boat.

"Help!" Peter shouted.

The man at the oars quickly turned on his seat. A look of shock crossed his face, and he reached two wiry arms down for Peter. The wooden edge of the boat scraped Peter's ribs as he climbed over the side. He was so exhausted he could hardly move.

"My friend," Peter said weakly. "There's a girl. She was with me just a minute ago, and now I can't find her!" He managed to sit up and point to the choppy water.

"A girl?" the man said, sounding anxious. He, too, gripped the edge of the boat, searching. Then he shouted, "Tunie! Tunie, are you out here?"

Peter stared. This man knew Tunie?! Then he heard a squeak and realized that Perch was in the boat, too!

"Her name is Dorothy," Peter said, but even as he spoke the words, he felt time sliding away too quickly. She had to come up for air or she'd drown. Where was she? The moon was bright, but the churning surface of the water obscured their view of anything underneath.

Suddenly there was a great turmoil by the boat, and in a surge of white, bubbling water, Dorothy appeared, seemingly thrust upward from below.

"Dorothy!" Peter cried. The man in the boat grasped her arms.

Then, to Peter's shock, he spied two eyes glowing under the water. Perch swooped near them and shrilled.

"Horus?!" How had the mummy gotten here? As the man lifted Dorothy, limp and sopping wet, in his arms, Peter reached over and clasped the small, mummified hand that was stretching out of the water. Horus weighed almost nothing, but it still took an incredible effort to hoist him into the boat.

Dorothy coughed, spewing seawater, and opened her eyes.

"She's alive!" Peter said. He started to cry, and Dorothy, catching sight of him, began to sob, too.

"It's okay," said the kind stranger. "You're all right now. You're all right."

The two children hugged the man, and Peter kept his arm tightly around the mummy, too.

"Thank you," Peter said to his rescuer. "Tunie's on a ship, headed that way." Peter pointed in the direction he thought the ship had sailed. "We need to get to her quickly. The kidnappers are still on board." Perch squeaked his agreement.

Peter took in their small wooden dory with the splintery oars.

"We'll never catch up to their boat in this," he said bleakly.

Horus, who'd been squinting at the horizon, perked up. "Look!"

Peter did. "A boat!"

The outline of a large yacht was plowing across the waves. It would pass them in minutes.

George picked up a lantern from the bottom of the boat. "Kids, hold this while I light it. Quick!"

Peter held the glass lantern while George fumbled open its doors and lit it. Once it was glowing, George lifted the lantern high over his head, swinging it back and forth.

"Over here!" he shouted in a loud voice. "We're here! Over here!"

Horus and Peter and Dorothy all joined in, yelling.

At first it seemed the yacht hadn't noticed them, but then, sure enough, it shifted.

"It's changing course!" Peter said.

Dorothy sat up straighter. As the yacht drew closer, they saw lanterns illuminating several men on board. Dorothy cried out with delight.

"Daddy! Daddy, is that you?" she called across the few feet of water that separated their boats, her voice shaking with emotion.

"Dorothy?!" For a moment, it looked as if the man would leap over the wooden rail in his desperation to reach his daughter.

"Wait, sir. We'll bring them up," said a sailor, keeping a hand on Mr. James's arm.

A rope ladder was unfurled down the side of the yacht, and the small group on the dory climbed up, one by one. Perch rode on Peter's shoulder. Horus came last and stood near enough to Peter to be his shadow. Nobody noticed the mummy.

Dorothy's father dropped the kerchief he'd been gripping and clasped Dorothy to him in a tight embrace, saying "My girl" over and over.

"Are you okay?" he asked finally. "Are you all right?"

"Yes," Dorothy said, weeping. The two clutched each other for a moment, while the rest of the crew gave Peter a towel and shook George's hand. The dory was hauled aboard and secured.

Peter spied Officer Hill and said, "Tunie's still on the boat with our kidnappers," he said.

Mr. James straightened, keeping his hands on Dorothy's shoulders.

"Let's get those animals," he said fiercely.

"I know the way," said Peter.

Beside him, Horus whispered, "Hang on, Tunie. We're coming."

The swift yacht sailed off in pursuit.

CHAPTER 40

Tunie sat in the dark with her knees tucked up toward her chest, her stomach lurching. She hoped she wouldn't be seasick; the sound and smell would lead Reid right to her. Where Tunie hid, it was stuffy and utterly black. She couldn't see a thing. Somewhere down below her, near the ship's metal hull, she heard a scrabbling sound. Rats, she supposed. She got gooseflesh thinking of them and hoped they would not crawl up the netting to where she sat.

She kept her breathing as quiet as she could, swallowed against her rising nausea, and concentrated on listening for Reid. She'd lost him again.

All at once, Reid's nasal voice sounded out of the gloom.

"I know you're in here," he said. He didn't sound far away, but it was hard to tell in the blackness. "I'll find you sooner or later. In fact, I'm thinking later. We won't get to port for two weeks. How long do you think you'll survive locked in here?" He laughed. "I can see the headline now: 'Poor Stowaway, Too Stupid to Bring Along Food or Water, Perishes in Hold of Ship.' What a pity. Not that anyone in the Caribbean will particularly care. Certainly, I won't. I will sit beneath the palms and lift my drink to toast your end. Ta-ta!"

With that, his footsteps receded. The hatch slammed shut. She heard a sound like metal scraping across it.

Tunie released the breath she'd been holding. Had he really left, or was this all a trick? She decided she'd sit still, a whole day if she could, to make sure. Better not to risk anything.

For nearly an hour, she sat unmoving in the dark, listening to the rats scrabble and the sounds of feet overhead, the water against the hull.

Then it happened. Again she felt the itching, feathery feeling in her nose, that searing buildup that made her eyes water. She pressed her tongue to the roof of her mouth, trying to suppress the sneeze, but it was no use.

"Ah-chooo!"

Instantly a match flared.

To her right, not six feet away, she saw the orange flame rise and ignite a lantern. Its glow brightened to reveal a gaunt face, curled mustache, and those cruel and terrifying dark eyes. Reid.

Tunie tried to scoot away, but Reid grabbed an ankle and yanked, tugging her toward him and raking her back painfully across the wooden corners of the crates.

"Argh!" Tunie cried out. She kicked at him with her other foot, hard, and accidentally connected with the lantern. It went flying. The space darkened, and she heard the sharp shattering of glass.

Reid clawed at her, trying to grab her other foot. Something behind him lit up. The smell of smoke reached Tunie's nose.

"Fire!" she shouted, gesturing behind Reid.

He turned, spied the fire, and swore, then abruptly released Tunie. He tore off his coat and tried to smother the flames, but the fabric ignited, too. Tunie ran over and stomped on the fire, but it was no use.

Reid looked wild. He put his hands to the sides of his head.

"My ship!" he cried. "We need water!"

She scrambled after him as he ran for the ladder, but he reached the hatch before her. As he hurried out, the hatch overhead closed with a click. Tunie climbed up the ladder and pounded on it. It was stuck. She hammered harder with her fists.

"Hey! It's locked!" Tunie shouted. "*Hey!*"

Gray-white smoke was rising up from the blaze. She

could see the fire growing, the flames leaping from crate to crate.

Tunie shoved against the metal hatch. She knocked on it with her fists.

"Can anyone hear me? Help! Fire!"

The smoke burned her lungs and made her eyes water. The cargo hold was becoming warm. Tunie coughed, banging continuously on the hatch overhead.

"Let me out! There's a fire!"

She glanced down. Through the fog of smoke, she could see the flames spreading across the wooden pallets lining the floor, toward the ladder. She was trapped. What was taking Reid so long?

The air was stifling. Darkness seeped in Tunie's periphery, blocking out the edges of her vision.

In a strangled voice, she called out, "Help! Someone!"

It sounded weak. She beat her fists against the hatch, but her arms were growing tired. She doubted anyone above deck would hear her.

Suddenly the hatch flung open. A policeman's head appeared, and the officer hauled her out, shouting for help.

"I found her! There's a fire! Sound the alarm!" It was Officer Hill. In moments, the crew was in action.

Tunie retreated with Hill, while the sailors formed a human chain, passing buckets of seawater down to those courageous enough to battle the conflagration in the hold. Both Tunie and Hill tried to keep out of the way.

Hill led her across the deck. Tunie spied a yacht waiting there.

"Thank you, Officer Hill," Tunie said as they walked. "You saved my life."

He shook his head, looking bewildered.

"Would you believe it—a bat showed me the way! It flapped around my head until I chased it down, and then it stopped and stood right there on the hatch, tapping its little claws on it like a bloomin' dancer and looking at me! When I got close, I heard you!"

"A bat? Where is it now?" Tunie looked around for Perch. She whistled for him, and out of nowhere the exhausted bat appeared. Perch gave a squeak of relief and landed on Tunie's forearm. His tiny claws gripped her sleeve and he swung upside down, falling instantly asleep.

Officer Hill looked on in shock.

"My little friend," Tunie whispered to Perch, blinking tears from her eyes. "What would I do without you?"

"TUNIE!" A boy's voice sounded from the nearby cruiser. Peter jumped over the gap between the vessels and came running toward her. He and Tunie embraced.

"You're alive!" Tunie said. She stepped back and spied Dorothy standing with her father, Mr. James, whom she recognized from the newspaper. Beside Mr. James stood . . . her neighbor?

"George?!" Tunie said. Before she could ask him anything, there was a commotion among the crowd on the steamship deck. An officer propelled Reid before him. Reid's wrists were handcuffed and he leaned back, resisting as the officer pushed him forward.

"It wasn't me!" Reid protested. "It was Detective Shade! All of it! I was planning to turn him in and free the kids when I had a chance!"

"You mean us?" Dorothy said angrily, standing tall.

Reid looked up and saw Dorothy, Peter, and Tunie flanked by a group of irate-looking policemen.

"He's lying," Dorothy said to the police.

Reid was doing his best to look surprised.

"I'm so happy to see you kids!" Reid lied. "I was only going along with him until I had a chance to get you away."

"He was chasing me down five minutes ago," Tunie said flatly to Officer Hill. "He and Shade kidnapped us and locked us in trunks."

While Reid was protesting, another officer appeared, shoving along the rumpled Detective Shade.

"Found this guy locked in a trunk. He tells me this kidnapping was all Reid's idea."

Shade and Reid started shouting curses at one another.

"I've heard enough," said Hill with disgust. He and Lovejoy began to march Shade and Reid onto Mr. James's yacht. "I know some fellow officers who'd like a word with you, ex-detective," Officer Hill said meaningfully to Shade.

Dorothy was busy talking to her dad and the police. Peter grabbed Tunie's hand and pulled her after him.

"I know a great place to sit," he said to Tunie. She was puzzled but let him lead her to the front of Mr. James's motor yacht.

Soon she realized why. Standing there, with his little wrapped hands grasping the rail and his head turned up toward the stars, was Horus.

"Horus!" Tunie cried. The slight, somewhat bedraggled mummy turned and stretched his arms out to her, a wide bandage smile on his face. Tunie ran up and clasped the little mummy to her chest as hard as she dared. The mummy returned her hug.

"Horus! You're ... you're here!" Tunie's eyes brimmed with tears.

"I'm extremely glad you're all right." Horus sounded hoarse with emotion. He wiped at his eyes.

"You must have done something wonderfully good!" Tunie said to him.

"What do you mean?"

Tunie leaned back, swallowed against the tears, and smiled.

"I found something in a curse book, a way to mitigate your curse. I was coming to tell you when Reid kidnapped me! I'll explain, but first you must report to me about everything," Tunie said. "I want a complete description of the last twenty-four hours. Don't leave anything out."

She sat on the bench beside Peter and Horus. While the watchful adults hovered nearby, seeing only Tunie and Peter and a small gap between them, the three friends sat together and talked all the way back to the harbor, pausing every now and then to admire the stars.

CHAPTER 41

Three months later, sunbrowned and travel weary, Peter looked through the window as his train slowly pulled into Harbortown Station. He spied his dad standing on the platform. Peter grinned, waving at his father, who appeared as tousled as ever. His dad's whole face transformed with happiness when he saw Peter. He waved back exuberantly.

The camp counselor sitting beside him shook Peter's hand. Peter stood up. The counselor was staying on the train, continuing up to Vermont, where he was from.

"See you next summer, Peter!" he said. "Can't wait to see what you engineer in the meantime. Send me sketches!"

Peter grinned. "You bet. See you next year!"

He descended the stairs, with his camp bag slung over his shoulder, and made his way through the crowd.

"Look at you!" Mr. Bartholomew said, embracing Peter tightly. He stood back and looked over his son, smiling. "You must be two inches taller! Camp seems to have agreed with you."

Peter couldn't stop smiling. "It was even better than I'd hoped."

His father's dark eyes looked a little wet beneath his glasses. He blinked. "I'm glad it was fun, but I'm pleased you're back. I can't wait to see what you made!"

As they walked the busy brick sidewalks to the bridge, Peter told his father about his bunkmates, their hikes, the battle robots they'd designed, and the final match between them on the last day of camp.

Peter chuckled, describing the robot face-off. "One kid, Charlie, installed a trip stick on his automaton—a length of pipe that popped out, whirled around, and knocked over all the others—but it knocked itself off balance, too. His robot started tumbling away in a zig-zag. Charlie chased after it all the way to the creek and fell in! It was pretty funny."

They'd arrived at their brownstone.

His father looked happy but wistful. "Well, did you have such a good time that you're sad to be home?"

Peter stood on the bottom step as his dad opened the door.

"Nah. I missed you and Tunie and Perch," Peter said. *And Horus,* he thought. He was looking forward to seeing the little mummy again. "I'd like to go again next year, though."

Peter's dad nodded. "Good. Miss Cook and Stepma arranged a little surprise for you."

He followed his dad into the wallpapered parlor. There sat Stepma holding baby Lucy, and the twins, both looking glum with their damp hair plastered neatly to their heads. Stepma smiled.

"Welcome home, Peter! We've missed you." She set the baby on the settee and stood up, giving Peter a genuinely warm smile and hug. Surprised, Peter hugged her back. He found he was glad to see her, too.

"Miss Cook baked you this." She waved to a chocolate cake, decorated with whipped cream and strawberries, resting on a silver platter on the coffee table. "She said it's your favorite."

Randall said in a petulant undertone, "*We* never get dessert before dinner."

Larry elbowed him.

"Wow, thanks," Peter said. "Wait, first—I made something for baby Lucy."

Peter dug through his camp bag. "Here."

He held up a wooden base that had a short metal pole with a carved, green-painted frog on top. He wound the toy up and set it in front of Lucy. The frog jumped back and forth, moving its legs and making a little bell sound. Lucy squealed and clapped her hands with delight.

Stepma gave Peter a loving look. "Why, it's wonderful, Peter! And very thoughtful. Thank you."

Peter turned to the twins. It was strange; seeing them now, all slumped and sulky, he could hardly believe he'd ever been afraid of them.

"I have something for you, too. Wait until you see."

He pulled out two windup toys, two-inch knights astride funny, stocky horses. Each knight held a lance.

"You wind them up and set them at each other, and whichever knocks the other over wins. We bet penny candy on our battles at camp. These won a lot."

He wound up the horses, and they moved across the floor with impressive speed and a loud clicking sound. One knocked the other over, and the horse spun around and around, its legs moving back and forth until it stopped. The rough-and-tumble toys had reminded him of the twins.

"Not bad," said Larry, his furry blond brows upraised. Peter handed one to him and the other to Randall.

"I'm working on a bigger version," Peter said. He looked to his dad and Stepma. "I haven't thought of anything for you two yet, but I will."

Stepma was watching baby Lucy, still enthralled by the ticktocking frog.

"This is present enough," she said.

"Indeed," his father agreed.

Everyone ate the cake down to crumbs, and finally Peter went to his room to unpack. He took WindUp out of the bag and set him on the bed.

"Well, we're home," Peter said to him quietly. He sat down on the creaky mattress and looked around his familiar room. Shortly there was a knock on the door.

Larry and Randall came into Peter's bedroom, carrying their windup knights.

Peter wasn't sure what they'd come to do until Larry said, "Uh, we were wondering what else you made."

"Oh." Peter rifled through his things and took out a small trebuchet. "This. We launched marshmallows at each other over the campfire and tried to catch them in our mouths. I still have some, I think." He looked through his bag and found a paper sack of marshmallow squares. "Sit over there," Peter said to Randall. Then he showed Larry how to work the trebuchet. The marshmallow square flew and softly bounced off Randall's face.

"Let me try!" Randall said. The boys took turns for a while.

Then Larry said, "I'll be right back."

While he was out of the room, Randall and Peter fired marshmallows at each other.

"How was it while I was gone?" Peter asked.

Randall lifted one big shoulder. "Boring. Mom said it was our fault you left."

Peter thought for a moment. "I guess that's partly true, but I wanted to go to camp anyway."

"Oh." Randall looked down at the trebuchet.

Larry returned, holding a sack from the drugstore. He handed it to Peter. Peter opened it. Inside was a new toothbrush.

Larry gestured vaguely in the direction of the bathroom.

"Because the other one's no good anymore," he said gruffly.

Peter had already bought a new toothbrush before camp, unwilling to use the shaving cream–flavored one in the bathroom. He didn't say that to Larry, though. He realized this was Larry's way of apologizing.

"Thanks" was all Peter said.

Stepma's voice sounded in the hallway. "Come down for dinner, boys!"

Peter made a face. "Bleh, I'm not hungry at all."

"Me neither," agreed Larry, but they all trooped downstairs together.

CHAPTER 42

Tunie wiped a drip of paint from her cheek and glanced through the open window at the clock inside the house.

"Oh!" she said. "We have to go!"

Her father smiled at her from his chair in the shade on the far side of the clearing. He'd been watching the masons repair the crumbling chimney while he ate a sandwich. With the reward money, they had plenty to eat. His cheeks weren't as skeletal as they'd been, pink now from sun, not fever, thanks to his doctor and medicine.

Mr. James had given a reward to their neighbor George, too, for his role in Dorothy's rescue. Tunie, Peter, George, and Dorothy had had their photograph taken together earlier in the summer, and it had appeared in the *Harbortown Gazette* under the headline KIDNAPPED GIRL RESCUED!

"Have a good time," her dad called over. "Tell Peter we're bringing dessert tomorrow."

"I will!" Tunie quickly untied the smock she'd put on over her clothes. She was painting the outside of their house a sunny yellow. Over the front door she'd hung up the beautiful gift Horus had given her—a picture he'd created on wood. On it were gorgeous, stylized hieroglyphics that Horus said spelled out *kindness*. Her mother would have loved it.

"Perch!" Tunie called. "Time to go. I know you hate the heat, but the library will be cool."

Perch flew down from the rafters, and the two set off at a trot.

The September sun was hot. On the streets, Tunie walked by men wearing banded, light-colored hats to keep the sun off their heads, and women in short-sleeved dresses. She stopped at an intersection to wait for a fire truck with spoked wheels and a ladder to pass, then crossed to the library.

Horus was waiting outside on the steps, bouncing up and down on his toes, his eyes bright and a child's red knapsack on his back.

"Hi, Horus!" Tunie said breathlessly. His joyous expression made her smile.

"Tunie! Guess what I've discovered?"

"What?"

"*Iced* tea. It's tea, made quite cold on purpose, for the greater enjoyment of drinking it in warm weather. Isn't it brilliant? I've brought a thermos of it for our picnic. I hope Peter remembers to bring something to sit on."

"Where is Peter?" Tunie asked.

The mummy scanned the pedestrians on the busy street.

"I can only assume he's late as well. Getting here took longer than I expected. These books I need to return are extremely heavy." He pointed happily to the bulging backpack.

"Let me guess," Tunie said warmly. "More mysteries?"

"Mysteries!" the mummy echoed with delight. "I can't get enough of them! Or nougat," he added. "I brought some of that, too."

"Yummy," said Tunie. She'd noticed that since the night they found Dorothy, Horus didn't carry around his sling stone anymore. She'd seen it in its display case, but as far as she could tell, Horus left it there, beneath the glass.

"There he is!" Tunie said, seeing Peter pelting across the street with WindUp peeking out of his knapsack, something long and red clutched in one hand.

"You made it," Tunie said to Peter as the three friends started up the steps to the library.

"I was busy finishing something for you and Perch," Peter gasped, handing Tunie the red item. Beneath his summer freckles, he was flushed.

It was a parasol. When Tunie opened it up, a small trapeze unfolded, hanging down from the spokes. With a happy squeak, Perch, who'd been awkwardly clutching Tunie's bag, flew up and hung from the bar.

"It's perfect!" Tunie said, genuinely pleased. "It will keep us cool and give Perch a way to ride. Thanks, Peter!"

"Glad you like it."

Tunie rested the parasol on her shoulder. "How are things with the twins? Still grand?"

Peter laughed. "I wouldn't say grand. I'd say . . . peaceable."

"Good enough," Tunie said.

They walked through the wide double doors of the library and followed a gray staircase to the lower level.

Peter glanced down at Horus.

"Horus, I have some ideas for you, too, but I need you to come over for some measurements. Later tonight?"

Horus nodded excitedly. "I have thoughts about gear you could fashion, too. Just think—now that I'm mobile, and invisible, I would make an excellent spy! Only for the right cause, of course."

Since Horus had helped rescue Tunie on the night of the full moon, he'd found he was free to leave the museum whenever the building was closed. During operating hours he was still trapped, but every evening and on Saturday afternoons when the museum closed at three— like today—he was free to roam. The children were having a great time introducing him to modern marvels. Though centuries old, Horus was a kid at heart and was making up for his lost childhood with gusto. He still, however, loved books most of all.

Tunie smiled affectionately at the mummy. "A spy! That's an ace idea! The library's closing pretty soon. Let's talk about it when we have our picnic on the roof."

The friends split up. Tunie made her way to the aisle of art books. She and her dad would occasionally make their mother's favorite drink—lemonade with mint— and look at the books together, picking out paintings they thought Tunie's mother would have liked. After Tunie told Peter about this, he and his father had a conversation about Peter's mom. They started doing something similar, but with music.

Next Tunie stopped by the mystery section—Horus's enthusiasm had proven contagious. The mummy wasn't there. Tunie selected a stack of mysteries, checked out everything, and made her way upstairs.

Among the small study areas on the top floor, Peter had discovered a small metal door with a broken latch.

"It seems to be my talent," Peter had said the first time they opened it. The door led to the rooftop. The view of the city from the library roof was the most spectacular any of them had seen. They could gaze out over the shining river in the distance, the busy, wending streets, the rows and rows of brick buildings stretching for acres. Up on top of the library, the sky was limitless. It was Horus's favorite place in the city. Saturday-evening sunset picnics had become their tradition. Because the library closed while they were on the roof, they always took the fire escape down.

Tunie shouldered her new parasol, with Perch clinging to its end, and stepped out onto the roof. She could see Horus and Peter had already spread out the blanket. Horus was pouring tin cups of iced tea, and Peter was taking sandwiches out of a metal lunchbox. She could hear him telling Horus about his latest invention.

"It's a water robot, a little friend for WindUp. Dorothy wrote and said I can test it in her pool next weekend when they're back from her grandparents' house." He touched the top of WindUp's head, and the robot emitted a cheery chime.

The evening was clear and mild. Tunie paused, looking at her two friends chatting and laughing. Behind them, the sky was growing pink. Horus's eyes reflected the orange light of the sinking sun. Tunie felt full of a similar radiance, warm and weightless. She left the doorway and walked toward them.

"I found you," she said.

ACKNOWLEDGMENTS

I'd like to extend heartfelt thanks to my terrific agent, Mary Cummings, for her hard work and valuable manuscript advice, and to Betsy Amster for taking such good care of me. Thanks also to Allison Wortche and Karen Greenberg for believing in this story and greatly improving it with their excellent and incisive editorial skills. Lastly, thanks to my husband for the endless readings and rereadings, and to my parents and siblings for their lifelong encouragement. I am the luckiest.